THE HAUNTING

Look for all the books in
THE HOUSE ON CHERRY STREET
trilogy:

THE HAUNTING
BOOK I

**RODMAN PHILBRICK
AND LYNN HARNETT**

AN
APPLE
PAPERBACK

SCHOLASTIC INC.
New York Toronto London Auckland Sydney

For Erin, Peter, Liza, and Lauren

ISBN 0-590-25513-4

12 11 10 9 8 7 6 5 4 3 2   5 6 7 8 9/9 0/0

Printed in the U.S.A.   40

First Scholastic printing, June 1995

1

You could see the house on Cherry Street from a distance. The old place was high up on a hill, surrounded by tall, whispery pines. As my dad turned the station wagon into the long driveway, I stuck my head out the window for a better look.

We'd be spending the whole summer here, and I was dying to know what was in store for me and my family. Mom and Dad and my kid sister Sally.

For a moment the house passed out of view, hidden behind the trees, and long shadows passed over the station wagon.

It was as if the sun had been erased from the sky.

"Well, there's certainly plenty of shade," said my mom doubtfully.

"And don't forget there's a lake at the other end of Cherry Street," said my dad, trying to sound cheerful.

Right then we came out of the shadows and

suddenly there it was, much closer this time, looming over us.

The house.

The sun glinted off the windows, winking and flashing through the tree branches. So bright it was like looking into a flame. As we rolled up the driveway the whole house finally came completely into view. It was a rambling, gabled old place with a wide front porch. The porch roof sagged slightly and the house needed painting, like nobody had taken care of it for a long time.

It was easily the biggest house on Cherry Street. The other places we passed were all one- or two-story summer cottages, small and plain-looking. This was a real house, almost a mansion.

I was staring up at the second floor, wondering if we'd be able to see the lake from there, when I saw something strange.

Something was there in the house. Something was watching us.

"Hey, did you see that!" I said, pointing. "Someone looking at us from the upstairs window."

"Maybe the cleaning lady is still here," Mom said.

"Or a trick of the sunlight reflecting off the glass," Dad said, easing his foot off the brake. "It doesn't look like anyone's been here in quite a while."

Yeah, right. They always think I'm imagining stuff, but I know what I saw. Someone was there,

2

and it wasn't a trick of the light. I searched the windows for another glimpse of the shadowy figure, but it was gone.

That's when my little sister Sally stirred, waking from her nap. She started squirming around in her seat belt, looking for attention. "There yet?" she asked. "There yet?"

Sally's just turned four and she'd been asking "There yet?" for the whole trip.

I told her we'd finally made it, and she started peppering me with a bunch of questions, but I wasn't really paying attention. I was thinking about what had been looking at us from the window. I'd only seen it for a moment, couldn't tell if it was a man or a woman or even a child. The shape had had a shimmery quality, and I might have thought Dad was right about a trick of the light if it hadn't been for the eyes. Because the thing in the window had eyes. Eyes that had bored right into me.

And now all the windows of the house seemed to be turned toward our station wagon, staring, sizing us up.

"Mommy, are we really there yet?" said Sally. She was wide-awake and fidgeting now.

"Yes, honey. Wait till Daddy stops the car before you take off your seat belt."

I leaned over and straightened out Sally's T-shirt and she giggled and gave me a big grin. I hear some guys complain about having little sisters, but Sally is cool even if sometimes she is a pain, always asking questions and repeating stuff until your head aches.

The old garage looked locked up, so Dad parked the wagon by the side of the house.

"Oh, look," Mom said. "A cherry tree."

The cherry tree was close to the side of the house, almost like it was growing out of the house somehow, and the branches were full of small pink blossoms.

"Isn't it late in the year for a cherry tree to be in bloom?" asked Mom of no one in particular.

Dad cranked down his window and took a deep, satisfied breath. "Just smell that fresh air," he said.

"Jason, would you — "

But I was already out of the car and running for the front door. Looking around, I realized you couldn't see any other houses from here. It was like we were all alone in the woods.

It was a neat old house, that was for sure, and I couldn't wait to see the inside. So I sprinted up the porch steps like an Olympic hurdler and reached for the front doorknob.

Out of nowhere a blast of cold air hit me. I mean *cold* air, so cold I couldn't move. Air so cold it felt thick.

I gasped as the frigid stuff flowed down into my throat. It tasted of earth, moldy earth. It smelled of the grave.

4

Shivering, I realized it was blowing up at me from under the front door. From inside the house.

I started to take a step backwards. Only my feet wouldn't move. I was stuck there! And the awful cold was seeping though my T-shirt and shorts.

I could feel ice forming around my stomach, creeping up my spine, icy fingers reaching for my heart.

I tried to turn my head and yell but my neck had gone rigid.

I was frozen to the spot and getting colder by the second.

2

Someone clapped a hand on my shoulder.
It was my dad.

"Come on, Jay, give us a hand unloading the car, then you can explore all you want."

He reached past me and slipped a key into the lock.

The spell was broken. The icy grip had slipped away with my father's touch. I shrugged my shoulders, feeling the blood humming through my veins once more, warmth returning to my legs and chest.

What a relief! The cold, damp air was still coming up from under the door, though. The weird thing was that Dad, wrestling with the stiff lock, didn't seem to notice.

"Don't you feel it?" I asked.

"Feel what?"

"Cold air coming out through the door."

Dad made a face and shook his head. "Jason, it's a beautiful summer day." Suddenly he looked concerned. "Maybe you're coming down with a cold," he said.

"No way!"

Suddenly the lock clicked and the door sprang open. My dad bowed and said, "After you, my dear Alphonse," which is his idea of being funny.

I laughed despite myself and for a moment forgot all about the strange, cold air and what it had done to me. I could see only a little way into the house. The interior was dim and full of shadows.

Just looking inside made my stomach feel weird. It was as if time had been standing still inside the house. As if it was waiting for me to step over the threshold and set it going again.

"Go on, Jay. What's wrong?"

"Uh, nothing," I said, and stepped through the door.

Behind me Dad said, "I'll go help your mother unpack the car. Have a quick look around and then give me a hand."

Which left me alone inside the house. The weird feeling that had come over me made me think something bad was going to happen, but it didn't.

Once I was inside, the house seemed okay. What was I thinking, that time had stopped inside? Maybe I really was reading too many scary books, like my mom is always saying.

There was nothing to be frightened of, old houses always looked a little spooky, right? So I went a few feet into the hallway. Sunlight poured over my shoulder and made it so you could see the dust hanging in the air. Like a mist over everything.

The entryway was a wide hall with a long curving stairway leading to the second floor. On one side of the entryway was a living room. I looked through an archway and saw a large formal dining room with tall, stern-looking chairs around a long dark table.

"Why, it's beautiful, charming!"

That was my mom, coming in behind me. She was carrying Sally in one arm and holding a suitcase with the other, which reminded me that I was supposed to help unload the station wagon.

I ran back to the wagon and grabbed two of the biggest suitcases. I'm average size for twelve, but strong, and the suitcases weren't any problem, except where I had to hump them up over the front steps. I was so hot and sweating from all the work that I never even thought about what had happened with the cold air.

My mom had let up all the shades and sunlight slanted in through the tall windows. The living room looked shabby but ordinary. There was an old couch and a couple of old chairs and end tables standing on an ugly round rug.

Next to the stairway the hall narrowed and

became a passage into the innards of the house. My mom's voice came from somewhere down there.

"Dave, come see," she called excitedly to my father. "There's a room here big enough for us to use as an office!"

I went back and got the last two suitcases and lugged them into the entryway. There! Nobody could say I wasn't carrying my weight around here. I straightened up, stretching my tired muscles.

Light filtered down the front stairway from the rooms above. But somehow I didn't feel ready to go up there just yet.

My parents were rumbling around upstairs. Mom sounded delighted with the place. Obviously they hadn't found anyone strange lurking in the house.

I looked up as Mom and Dad came back down the stairs. Their progress was slow, since they were letting Sally set the pace. The sunlight caught in my mom's wavy blond hair, making it shimmer like a crown.

"All this place needs is a good airing," said Mom, dimples showing on either side of her broad smile. "But we'll have to be careful of the furniture. Some of these pieces are quite valuable. Like that living room rug."

A valuable rug? Was she serious? The thing was mouse-colored and threadbare. I didn't say it out

9

loud, but it looked like somebody had puked all over it. Definitely.

Mom loved it. "It must be eighty or a hundred years old," she said enthusiastically. "And hand-made. Maybe we should roll it up, Dave. Store it in the basement or the attic."

Dad shook his head. "It's too delicate. I'd be afraid the threads would tear. We'll just have to be civilized." He caught sight of me and smiled. "You hear that, Jay? No eating in the living room and no muddy sneakers."

"Jason! Did you do all this?" asked Mom, sur-veying the line of suitcases. "That's sweet of you, dear, but we didn't mean for you to do everything. Why don't you run upstairs and take a look at your room. It's the one on the left at the top of the stairs."

It was now or never. I took a deep breath, grabbed my suitcase, and took the stairs two at a time.

"Careful putting your clothes away," Mom called up after me. "That dresser is a valuable antique."

I skidded into the room on the left and dropped my suitcase. The room was awesome. It had ceil-ings so high you could set up a basketball hoop. There were two big windows that looked out over the backyard. One of the windows was recessed into a dormer, a little alcove with a window seat.

Cool. I knelt on the cushioned bench of the window seat and leaned forward to look out the window. The yard sloped down the hill toward the lake. Or that's what I figured, even though you couldn't see the lake because of all the trees.

I swiveled around from the window and checked out my new bedroom for the summer. All this space! And hardly any furniture. Just a bed set high off the floor with four tall posts and a tall wooden headboard, a rickety old dresser (*that* was the antique?), and a beat-up old table that would be perfect for gluing up airplane models on rainy days or whatever.

There was a full-length mirror on the closet door. I grinned into it and it grinned right back at me. The mirror was old and kind of spotty and made me seem about twice as tall, which looked neat, like I was an NBA basketball player. The problem was that stretched out I looked even skinnier than I really am. My legs looked like knobby sticks, especially in my baggy shorts, and my arms stuck out like toothpicks.

Dork city, definitely.

I bounced up and down in front of the weird old mirror a few times watching how a wave in the middle turned my body to rubber, and my ears wiggled like elephant flaps.

This was better than a funhouse and the admission was free, right in my own bedroom. After a while it got pretty boring, though, so I went back and checked out the window seat.

I took off the cushion and you could tell it was like a built-in toy box, and the seat part was the lid.

So open it up, Doofus, I told myself. See if there're any toys inside. But a funny feeling made me not want to open the lid.

Maybe there was something inside. Something that wanted to come out.

"Don't be ridiculous," I said out loud.

Then I reached out and flung open the lid.

The toy box was empty.

Whew! I let out the breath I'd been holding. What a complete goon I was being, afraid of an empty toy box!

I let the lid fall and started unpacking my suitcase. It's going to be a great summer, I thought, throwing my clothes into the old dresser hurriedly.

Suddenly I wanted to get unpacked and get outside, check out the neighborhood, and see if there were other kids my age.

The bottom drawer stuck. I reared back, ready to kick it, then remembered what my mom said about it being valuable. Which you'd never know to look at it, that was for sure!

Sighing, I got down on my knees and worked to loosen that stupid drawer. I jiggled it sideways and finally it came free with a piercing shriek of wood on wood.

I winced and let go of the drawer.

But the shriek went on. It got louder. More urgent.

Sally. My little sister was screaming. Screaming as if somebody — or something — was trying to hurt her.

3

I ran out into the hall. The scream was louder. It was definitely coming from up here on the second floor.

"Sally?" I hurried toward the sound, worried that Sally was really hurting and not just crying for attention like she sometimes does.

The crying was coming from a room at the far end of the hall. The door was closed.

"Sally?"

I opened the door and the sobbing stopped in mid-wail.

There was nobody in the room.

A child-sized chair rocked gently in the corner. Which really spooked me until I realized it must have been the force of my opening the door that got it started. Or these creaky old floors, totally uneven.

I started to leave when a movement outside the window caught my eye. Frowning, I took a step toward the window.

Sally! She was down there in the backyard chasing a beach ball and laughing like she never had a care in the world. What was going on here? The hairs prickled along the back of my neck.

Someone had been in this room, crying and screaming bloody murder.

And if it wasn't Sally, then who was it?

As I stood there like a dolt staring out the window, trying to get a grip on some kind of logic with my sluggish mind, I heard a loud banging noise coming from downstairs.

Someone was at the door, trying to get in.

"Hey, Mom!" I shouted. "Someone's at the door!"

No answer. Mom must be outside, looking after Sally. The pounding was making the walls shake and I decided I had better answer the door before the house fell down. So I sprinted down the hall, slid down the banister, and jumped off the end. That's when I realized the pounding wasn't coming from the front door like I'd thought. It was coming from the back door.

My throat felt thick, like it was hard to swallow. Why was everything so strange in this old house?

Go ahead, I told myself, answer the door.

I went into the kitchen. Nobody was there. The banging on the back door was deafening. Wham, wham, wham!

Somehow I knew it was a summons meant for me alone.

4

I gathered up my courage, grabbed the knob, and flung the door open.

There on the back steps was a round-faced kid with fat freckles and a gap-toothed grin.

"Hi! Jason? I'm Steve. From next door."

I stared at him, trying to smile back. Steve was a little shorter than me but husky and solid instead of beanpole skinny. He was wearing a Stephen King T-shirt and baggy shorts and looked about my age.

"Your mom said I should knock real loud since you were upstairs."

So that was it. Relieved, I stepped back from the door. "Come on in."

"I've never been in here before," said Steve, looking around the kitchen eagerly. "My family comes every summer but nobody ever stays in this house." Steve ducked his head as if he'd said too much. "Hey, do you play ball? There's not a whole lot of kids here but we might be able to get a game together — if you don't mind playing with girls."

"What do you mean, nobody ever stays here?" I demanded.

Steve avoided looking me in the eye. He shrugged and scuffed at the floor with the toe of his sneaker. "People don't, that's all."

"What's wrong with this house?" I asked.

Steve hesitated, like he didn't want to say any more. Right away I figured he had an active imagination, like they're always saying about me, and he was used to people not believing him.

"It's okay," I said. "You can tell me."

I grabbed a package of cookies from the counter and dropped into a chair at the kitchen table, kicking another one out for Steve. I opened the cookies and held out the package. "Tell me about this house," I said.

Steve sat down and helped himself to a fistful of Oreos. He broke one apart and ate it, inside first, while I waited, watching him. Steve sighed and leaned across the table. "OK. There was some people rented it last year. They had a couple of little kids, about the same age as your sister. I don't know anything except they left in the middle of the night and never came back."

"That's it?" I said.

Steve looked stung. He looked over his shoulder and leaned in close again. "There used to be an old lady lived here. All by herself for years and years. She had bedbugs in her attic, if you know what I mean. And she was mean — she hated kids, I guess." He sat back and reached for another cookie, looking pleased with himself. "I heard she died in here and nobody ever found the body." He grinned at me. "What do you say we look for it?"

The backdoor opened and sunlight fell across the table. "OK, guys, out of here." Mom came in and the first thing she did was confiscate the cookies. "I want to get the rest of our stuff unpacked and I don't need you boys underfoot."

"Sure, Mrs. Winter," said Steve, standing quickly. "I'll show Jason the lake."

Good idea. I needed to get out of that musty old house and clear my head.

"Wait a second," said Mom. "Put these empty boxes in the garage, will you?"

"Sure, Mom, no problemo."

The garage was this old, rickety building attached to the side of the house. When we'd first come up the driveway, the overhead door had been shut. Now it was wide open.

"What a mess," Steve said. "Look at all that neat old stuff."

The garage was dark — no windows — but I could make out all the old junk stacked inside. There hardly seemed to be room for any more empty boxes.

I stepped over a broken chair, making my way toward the rear of the building.

Steve followed. "All this junk must have belonged to the old woman," he said, picking up a battered lampshade. He lowered his voice to a spooky whisper. "I didn't tell you everything."

"Yeah, right." I rolled my eyes sarcastically but of course Steve couldn't see me in the gloom.

"No, really. She was a witch. And she really hated kids. Especially little kids. Of course, now that she's a ghost she has more power. She can do anything. Over the years lots of little children have disappeared from this neighborhood."

Right then I banged my shin on a rusted rake. "Ouch! You know what, Steve? I think you're making all this up. Give me a hand here."

"Am not," Steve protested as he helped me shove the empty boxes way up on a stack of junk.

"Yeah? Then prove it," I said. "Prove that this place is haunted."

Suddenly the garage door slammed shut.

It was as if the sun had winked out. The garage was instantly, totally, utterly dark.

"How'd that happen?" Steve whispered, his voice shaky.

"I don't know but let's get out of here."

I pushed past Steve and began to pick my way toward the front of the garage. I kept bumping into things and stumbling over old paint cans.

Finally my outstretched hands found the door. "I got it," I shouted, fumbling for the handle. "We're out of here!"

Behind me I could hear Steve letting out a long sigh of relief.

My fingers found the handle, turned and pulled. Nothing happened.

The door was locked. We were trapped.

5

"We gotta get out of here," said Steve, his voice rising.

Somewhere in all the mess something rustled.

"Was that you?" I said.

"Was what me?"

It came again, a scratching, scrabbling kind of sound. Whatever it was, it wasn't human.

"That's not me," said Steve. "I didn't move a muscle."

A cobweb brushed my forehead and I jerked my head away. You never know about poisonous spiders.

"I'll bet there's rats in here," I said. "That must be what's making that scrabbling noise. Rats."

Steve groaned in the dark. "Stop fooling around and open the door, Jason. It wasn't true what I said, I admit it, OK?"

Wasn't true? What was he talking about?

"About the old lady," said Steve. "I don't know

anything about any missing kids. Now get us out of here."

I should have been relieved that he was making it up, but something about the darkness put a creepy-crawly feeling in my stomach. Like there were shapes in the dark I couldn't quite see, or invisible hands reaching out to touch me.

Yeah, right. I was acting like a five-year-old, scared of the dark!

"Jason, get us out of here, OK?" Steve said. His voice was kind of high-pitched.

The darkness was getting to both of us.

We pounded on the door and shouted as loud as we could but no one came.

"It could be hours," I said dejectedly. "My mom's inside and my dad's probably helping her. They'll never hear us."

"Let's try again." Steve's breath sounded ragged.

I banged again on the door and shouted as loud as I could. Steve shouted even louder and banged on the wall. We were making so much noise we didn't hear the smooth click of the lock.

Suddenly the door opened and sunlight blinded us. I blinked and shaded my eyes, trying to make out the looming figure coming into the garage.

It was my dad, of course. Who else had I been expecting? Some made-up little old lady? Yeah, right.

"You boys stop your goofing around," my father said. "I've got too much to do to be watching out for you."

"We weren't fooling around," I insisted. "I was putting some stuff away for Mom and someone came along and shut the door. It wasn't you?"

"This is an old house," Dad said. "I don't want you horsing around and breaking something valuable or putting your foot through some rotten board and breaking a leg, understand?"

There's no point in arguing with my dad when he gets that tone. "Yes, sir," I said.

Steve didn't say anything until my father was gone.

"The 'rents never understand," he said.

"Rents?"

"Short for parents," he explained. "Anyhow, I'd just as soon forget about that stupid garage door. Maybe it was the wind or something."

"Maybe," I said. But there hadn't been any wind.

"It's great to have a guy my own age right next door," said Steve. "Hartsville's OK but there's not that many kids. How did you happen to come here?"

"My parents are architects," I explained. "They're designing Hartsville's new town complex. So this isn't a vacation for them. A real-estate agent found the house for us."

"Spooky house," said Steve as we walked under the tall pines. "Wouldn't it be neat if it was really haunted?"

"Yeah, right," I said. For some reason I didn't feel like joking about it. As we turned toward the house, I searched the upstairs windows but didn't say anything to Steve about whatever it was that had been watching me when we first arrived.

No way would he believe me.

"You play baseball?" he asked.

"Sure."

"Tell you what," Steve said. "Wait here and I'll go get my ball and glove. We can practice. I start junior high this fall and I want to be the ace pitcher."

Steve went home to get his stuff and I ran upstairs to get my own ball and glove.

Something made me stop at the top of the stairs. I don't know what — just a feeling. As if something was watching me. Something waiting for me to make some kind of mistake.

As if the old house itself was watching, waiting.

I shook off the feeling — don't be a total moron, it's only an old house — and grabbed my glove.

On the way back down the stairs I noticed a few shelves full of these little ornaments. Really fragile-looking vases and china figures and old glass bottles. Just running down the stairs made them vibrate and shake, and all of a sudden it came to me.

The place was chock-full of breakable old stuff, and my mom had made a big deal about how valuable some of it was — I knew I'd be in big trouble if stuff got broken somehow, even if I didn't do it on purpose. Maybe *that's* why I was so nervous and jumpy around the house.

Get a grip, Jason.

What I did was slow down and take the steps one at a time. Much better. Get used to the house and maybe it would get used to me.

Steve was waiting in the backyard, seeing how high he could chuck a ball straight up. Which was pretty impressive — he had a strong arm.

"Tell me if I throw too hard," he said, whipping the ball at me.

It stung, but I said, "Don't worry about throwing too hard. I know how to catch."

Me and my big mouth. Steve did a full windup and threw a fastball right at my head. I caught it in the web of my glove, so it didn't hurt that time, but he kept showing off and after about ten minutes my hand was so numb it almost didn't hurt anymore.

"Pretend like there's a batter at the plate," he said. "Signal where I should throw, inside or outside, high or low."

I signaled for a low and inside pitch, and what do you know, he did it perfectly.

I had figured Steve was just bragging about wanting to be the ace pitcher on his school team, but it turned out he was really good. A lot better than me, in fact. You had to pay attention or that fastball of his would take your head off.

I had to concentrate so hard that for a while I almost forgot about the house. That strange feeling it gave me. Then when we took a break, it was back.

We were sitting under the tree, taking it easy, when I felt it. A tingling sensation right between my shoulder blades. I tried to shake it off, like a pitcher shakes off a signal he doesn't like.

But still I felt it, a creepy tingle moving up to the back of my neck.

This was ridiculous! It was all those stories Steve had been telling me. I kept imagining what it would be like to stumble on the old lady's skeleton under a pile of junk in the garage. Or what if I opened a closet and there she was.

Someone called out Steve's name.

"That's my mom, I gotta go," he said, getting up. "See you later, alligator."

"In a while, crocodile," I said right back. But my heart wasn't in it. All I could think about was the house — that something was wrong, something that might put me and my family in danger.

After Steve was gone I took a deep breath, gritted my teeth, and turned to look up at the building.

It was just a house. A big, rambling house with lots of windows and shadowy places, but just a house. Its windows were just glass. I stared at the place defiantly, my eyes traveling from one blank window to another, across the first floor, back across the second, up to the attic —

My heart slammed in my chest.

A small boy was there in the attic window. Watching me. Staring down at me.

A small, skinny boy with skin as pale as death.

6

I raced for the house and yanked open the kitchen door. I ran into the study, where my parents had set up their temporary office. There was a drafting table and rolls of blueprints and a couple of jars of sharpened pencils. Mom looked up from the worktable, where she was checking figures on her desktop computer. She smiled when she saw me.

"Hey, Jay, did you have fun with your new friend?"

"Mom," I said, catching my breath. "Did any little kids come into the house? A boy about Sally's age?"

She shook her head no, and I bolted for the hallway and ran up to the second floor.

It took me a few moments to figure out where the attic staircase was located. At the end of the hall, across from my bedroom, behind a narrow door.

As I went up, the attic steps groaned under my

feet — if I didn't know better I'd say it sounded almost human.

I got to the top and threw open the attic door.

It wasn't what I expected. Back home the attic is wide open, you can see from one end of the house to the other. But this attic was divided up into smaller rooms, one leading into another. Sort of like a maze.

It was strange, but as I went from one little room into the next, it seemed like I was walking for miles. Impossible, of course. It was just an old attic. It couldn't be miles long. No way. Maybe I was just tired from playing ball with Steve.

I tried to picture where it was I'd seen the little boy — what part of the attic he'd been in when he looked down at me from the window.

Had to be somewhere over here to the left.

I went through a door and found myself in a small room with no windows. Not the right room. But there was a small door at the other end of the room.

I pushed through the door and gasped in surprise.

Somehow I'd gotten completely turned around. This bare room had a window all right, but it seemed to be facing the wrong direction. Instead of looking over the backyard I was seeing out the front, toward the street and the tall pines.

How could I have messed up so badly?

I'd have to go back and start over. But which

way? My heart lurched as I realized this room also had two doors and I couldn't remember which one I'd entered.

Crazy. You couldn't get lost in your own house, right? Right?

When I finally decided which door to try, my feet moved like I was wearing lead boots. For some reason my heart started pounding hard against my ribs. I could hardly bring myself to reach out for the doorknob. But I did. I turned it, went through the door, and found myself in another small windowless room with a door opposite.

It was exactly like the room I'd just left. Weird. What was going on here? And why was I in a cold sweat? Why were my hands shaking?

Got to get out of here, I decided. Forget looking for that stupid kid. He could have this weird old attic and all these strange little rooms!

I turned back, opened the door I'd just come through.

And almost walked into a blank wall. It was a closet.

"Pull yourself together," I whispered to myself. "There has to be an explanation. You just got confused, that's all."

That's when I heard someone on the stairs. Someone was coming up into the attic. Whoever it was was trying to be quiet but the steps creaked and groaned.

"Dad?" I called out hopefully.

I heard the attic door open. Footsteps coming closer, very quiet.

"Mom? Sally?"

No response.

Just the footsteps shuffling closer and closer.

I started for the other door, wanting to get away from those creepy footsteps, and the door swung slowly shut, right before my horrified eyes.

Then the laughter started. Creepy laughter echoing through the maze of little rooms, bouncing from one to another.

It was the laughter of an evil witch at least a thousand years old.

I stood frozen to the spot as the shuffling footsteps came closer, closer, and the laughter rose and fell.

Closer and closer.

The doorknob rattled.

I pressed myself against the wall, staring at the closed door, my heart slamming so hard I thought it might jump right out of my chest.

The knob turned and rattled again.

The door started shaking, as if something big was outside, trying to get in. It shook so hard the screws started popping out of the hinges.

Now the floor was shaking, too.

I tried to grab hold of the wall as the whole room began to twist and buck. As if an earthquake was set on tearing it apart. Or as if the room itself was quaking in terror.

I fell to the floor and covered my head.

All around me the laughter rose higher and higher, louder and louder. An eerie, cackling noise filled my head and made me want to scream. But I clenched my teeth together — if I made any noise, whatever it was out there would know I was in the room.

Slowly the shaking subsided, but the laughter lingered right outside the door.

As quietly as possible I crawled and slid over to the closet. Something told me it wasn't over, and that I'd better hide. I got into the closet, eased the door shut, and crouched in a corner.

There, I was safe. It would never find me in here.

I waited in the darkness for what seemed like a long time. The laughter faded. Slowly my muscles began to unknot.

It's safe to come out, I thought. I started to get to my feet when I heard something enter the room.

Footsteps came slowly across the floor and stopped right outside the closet door.

It had found me.

7

"**J**ason? You up here?"

"Dad!"

Relieved beyond relief, I burst out of the closet and fell to my knees, gasping but happy.

"Jason, what's going on here? Is this some sort of game?"

"It's no game, Dad. There's something wrong with this house," I said. "It's — it's haunted!"

I told Dad about the boy I'd seen in the window, the violent shaking of the room, the eerie cackling. "You must have heard that spooky laughing," I added. "It was really loud."

My father shook his head slowly. "No, son, I didn't. I didn't hear anything but you crashing around up here."

"I swear I saw somebody up here. He was watching me."

My dad kind of smiled, as if he thought I was joking. "Tell you what, Jay. Let's you and me walk back through these rooms and see if anybody's up here."

As I followed my father back through the empty rooms, an odd thing happened. This time the attic didn't seem to be miles long, and in no time at all we'd checked out every single room.

No kid. No boy at the window. Nobody at all.

"You think I'm crazy, right?" I said.

Dad smiled and put his hand on my shoulder. "I think you've been reading so many of those scary books that your imagination has gotten the best of you. Think about it, Jason — you know there's no such thing as a haunted house."

"I guess you're right," I said. But in my heart I wasn't so sure. I'd seen the boy with the sad-looking eyes and the skin as pale as death. Like he'd just got up out of a coffin.

"Come on," Dad said, turning to leave. "You can give me a hand fixing that old clock in the hallway."

As we started back down the stairs, a door somewhere in the house slammed violently — BANG! — making us both jump.

Dad chuckled. "Now you've got me doing it," he said. "It's just the wind, Jason."

But I knew it wasn't the wind. There wasn't any wind at all. The air was as still as the grave.

8

The grandfather clock was as tall as my father — six feet. It stood beside the stairway in the hall between the living and dining rooms.

Dad knelt on the floor shining a flashlight into the works. I stood nearby so I could hand him stuff from his toolbox.

Helping my father is usually pretty cool because he knows what he's doing and he doesn't mind explaining. My mom says if he hadn't been an architect, he'd probably have been a teacher.

Normally I like giving him a hand. So how come I wanted to get away as fast as I could?

For some reason being near that big old grandfather clock made me feel out of breath. I didn't dare say so, not after what had happened in the attic. My dad would think I was losing my mind or letting my imagination run wild.

But it wasn't my imagination. The thing really did give me the creeps. For one thing the clock face looked way too much like a real face. A cold,

35

unfriendly face that watched me with some secret knowledge.

As if the clock could read my thoughts.

"I don't understand it," said Dad. He rocked back on his heels and frowned. "There's nothing wrong with the works or the springs. And I'm sure I've wound it correctly. But it just doesn't want to go." He clapped his hands on his knees and stood. "I give up. How about you put these tools away, buddy, while I wash up?"

"Sure, Dad." I gathered up his things and slipped each tool into its proper slot.

My eyes avoided the clock. But when I was finished putting the tools away, something made me whirl around to look at its face.

The hands of the clock had moved. And it had never even ticked. I felt a change in the air. The clock was definitely watching me. And waiting.

Something was about to happen, I could feel it.

Footsteps. I heard footsteps!

In the hall above me, running hard. A child's footsteps, hurtling headlong down the hallway.

And something larger in pursuit. Something gaining on the child, something big and bad.

I found myself silently rooting for the running child. "Come on, come on! Don't let whatever it is catch you!"

The running footsteps were coming closer, heading for the stairway landing. I ducked under the stairs and looked up at the landing. I wanted to yell for my dad but my breath was stuck in my chest.

I stared up at the landing, unable to blink as the pounding footsteps came closer, closer.

Then it screamed.

A loud, piercing shriek. I heard a small body hit the stair railing, hurtle over the top, and crash to the floor with a sickening thud.

Then came a silence. A terrible silence. A deadly, deadly silence.

I couldn't stand it anymore. I jumped out from under the stairs, expecting to see a dead body crumpled on the floor.

There was nothing.

No dead body. Nothing. There was nothing there at all.

Except for the shadows closing in. And the clock watching me. Watching and waiting.

9

That night I couldn't get to sleep.

The old house kept making noises in the dark. The walls creaked, the pipes moaned, the floorboards groaned.

Small animals scratched and scrabbled inside the walls. Or that's what it sounded like. Maybe it was just leaves brushing against the outside of the house.

Maybe.

While tossing and turning I worked out what had been happening to me all day. The thing was, I just wasn't used to old houses. In my neighborhood at home, normal sounds were stuff like cars going by, horns tooting sometimes, birds in the trees, people running lawn mowers and power tools.

Here you heard all kinds of stuff I wasn't familiar with. Probably I'd heard mice chasing each other in the walls and imagined a child running.

Then some old plumbing pipe hissed an air bubble and it sounded to me like a scream.

That must have been what happened.

That time when I thought Sally was crying? It was probably some neighbor's yowling cat or maybe the pipes again.

And the weird laughter in the attic? Obviously the wind moved through all those little rooms and gables in some odd way I wasn't used to.

It was a good thing my parents didn't know the half of it. They'd think I was acting like a two-year-old.

Anyhow, that's the kind of stuff I was thinking about. Instead of counting sheep, or whatever it is you do when you can't fall asleep, I was counting all the weird things that had happened the very first day in the house. The noises, the child crying, the strange little rooms in the attic, the shaking, the crazy laughter, the watching clock, the sound of a body falling . . .

Slowly I dozed off.

Hours later I woke up suddenly, my muscles rigid.

Where was I? It was dark, pitch-black. Then slowly it came back to me.

I was on summer vacation. This was my new room, my new bed. My first night in a strange house. Nothing to be afraid of, nothing at all.

I relaxed, wondering what had woken me up. A creaky noise? A squirrel in the attic? Had to be something like that.

Then I heard it. the grandfather clock chimed once, twice. Two A.M.

BONG. BONG.

The clock! I shot up off my pillow. The clock was supposed to be broken!

As soon as the second BONG faded, I heard a light, pitter-pattering sound in the hallway. Footsteps running past my door.

Was my kid sister Sally walking in her sleep?

The footsteps stopped, and I heard a creaking groan, as if the whole house was shuddering. Then a SHREEEEEEEEK! like a stubborn nail being pulled out of an old piece of wood.

Except it wasn't a nail. That shriek sounded as if it was coming from someone alive. Or maybe dead.

More little footsteps. There was a child out there. What if it was Sally? What if she was in trouble and needed my help?

I forced myself out of bed and felt my way across the room. When I was almost to the door the footsteps stopped as suddenly as they had started.

Whew! If that was really Sally out there, she'd gone back to her own room. Probably just sleepwalking. I sighed and turned from the door when I heard a skittering, scratchy sound.

Out in the hall. Something was moving around out there, dragging itself around.

SCREEEEEEEEEEE!

I jumped about a foot. That was the sound of nails being screeched along the wall — like fingernails on slate! The scratching noise was coming down the hall, getting closer and closer.

It stopped right outside my door.

I could hear ragged breathing. And then an old, creaky voice spoke to me through the door.

"Where is it?" the eerie voice hissed. *"Give it to me. It's mine. MINE!"*

I had two choices. I could either hide under the bed or open the door and see who was out there.

I'm thinking bed, absolutely, hide under the bed — but before I could make a move, the door slowly creaked open.

I stood there frozen. My whole body was tingling with fear. Something was coming into my room!

I took a deep breath, gathered up my courage, and jumped out into the hallway. With my fists up, ready to take a swing.

The hallway was empty. Except for the whispering.

A soft, whispering murmur came from the shadows. A whispering that seemed to move around, as if going from one dark corner to the next.

"Jayyyyyyy-ssssssssonnnnnnnnnn. Jayyyyyy-ssssonnnnnnn."

It knew my name.

Out of the corner of my eye I saw a flicker of movement in the shadows.

The whispery voice said, *"Jayyyyyy-ssssonnnnn. Give it to meeeeeeeeeeee!"*

I ran back into my room and slammed the door. I turned the key in the lock and waited, but nothing happened. Nobody tried to turn the handle or rattle the door. And the whispering had turned into the sound of wind.

Wind?

I turned. The window was open and the night breeze was making the curtains billow. Ghostly white curtains shivering in the moonlight.

Strange. Because the window had been closed when I left the room.

The breeze was cold. Bone-chilling cold. I went to the window. The curtains blew up around my face, touching me like cool, soft fingers. I shoved the curtains aside and tugged on the window.

It was stuck. It wouldn't close. The frame was big and heavy and the window wouldn't budge. I yanked it for a while and then gave up — I'd just have to wrap up in the blankets and hope it didn't get any colder.

I sighed and started to turn away from the stubborn old window when something made me look outside. The moon. There were clouds racing across the moon. Suddenly the clouds cleared from the sky and the moonlight cast long, wavery shadows from the tall trees.

Something was out there, moving among the trees. Trees that looked like tall soldiers marching against the night sky.

I stuck my head out the open window to see what it was. An animal? Maybe a deer, that would be cool, seeing a deer in the moonlight.

Somebody laughed. Somebody in the room right behind me.

It was an old, cackling voice.

I flinched, and as I did, I sensed the window moving above my head. I whipped my head out of the way. There was a searing pain and then BANG! the window came down like a guillotine blade.

If I hadn't moved it would have cut my head off! Or at the very least broken my neck.

I whirled around but the room was empty. Nobody there. Nobody at all.

Something caught my eye at the window. A lock of my hair caught in the sash where it had nicked my head on the way down. So close. So deadly.

It wanted to kill me. Something in this house wanted me dead.

10

The next time I woke up the sun was streaming in the window. It was going to be a warm summer day, but I shivered, remembering what had happened.

Or had it?

The room was so bright and cheerful, so totally normal, it made me wonder.

I decided it was Steve's fault, filling my head with all those creepy stories about an old lady who hated kids.

Suddenly the smell of bacon frying downstairs made my mouth water. I'd never been so hungry in all my life. I got dressed in a hurry, pulling on an oversized T-shirt and shorts.

I yanked on my baseball cap. Ouch! It was still sore where the window had grazed me. I checked out the little scrapy place on my scalp — proof that at least the falling window hadn't been imaginary.

Mom would say: You know better than to leave

an old window open without making sure it's propped up. Which is exactly why I decided not to tell her about it. No point in making a big stink until I had proof there was something wrong.

I ran downstairs hoping that my mom was making pancakes to go with the bacon.

Yes! Mom was at the stove, humming some old tune of hers and flipping a pancake. Sally, still wearing her pj's, was already chowing down at the table.

"Hi there, sleepyhead," Mom said.

"Morning, Mom. Where's Dad?"

"He had to deliver some blueprints to the job site. He'll be back soon."

"I could eat a horse," I said. "But I'll settle for about six pancakes."

"I expect this country air has given you an appetite," said Mom, turning to smile at me. "Were you the one who had the midnight munchies?"

"Huh?" I blinked at her stupidly.

"The corn muffins your father picked up yesterday," said Mom, cocking her head. "You must have been hungry to eat all four of them."

"I didn't eat any of them," I said. "I didn't even know we had corn muffins."

Mom frowned slightly, then shrugged. "It doesn't matter. They'll turn up probably. Do you think you can manage six pancakes?"

"Absolutely," I declared, pulling out a chair. "No problemo."

She narrowed her eyes at me. "I didn't hear you washing up before you came down."

"Ah, Mom."

She rolled her eyes. "You know the rules. Just because you're on vacation doesn't mean you don't have to wash up before meals."

It was no use arguing. With my stomach rumbling from near starvation, I dragged myself off to the downstairs bathroom.

This was the first time I'd really checked out the place. It was a small bathroom with very high ceilings and a lot of pipes running outside the walls, like they used to do in the old days. Instead of regular faucets there were these two bronze levers you pushed. I gave them a shove and stuck my hands under the spout. Barely a trickle of cold water came out. I frowned and gave the levers another hard push. The water sputtered and burped. Somewhere deep in the bowels of the house the pipes clanged loudly, making me jump.

Suddenly water gushed out, scalding hot. I jerked my hands away and jumped back from the sink as splashing droplets stung my legs.

"Darn!" The faucet was so hot to the touch I couldn't turn it off. I looked for a towel to use to protect my hands.

Just as I turned my head, the pipes along the wall burst, shooting hot water and steam right where my face had been a second before.

I let out a yell and leaped for the door, trying

to get away. The scalding water was spraying everywhere now and the room was filling with steam.

I grasped the doorknob. It wouldn't budge.

A stream of hot water hit me behind the ear and I screamed. My shoulders and back felt half-boiled. My bare legs burned.

And then I heard it. Someone laughing. A mean, cruel laugh that echoed through the steam-filled bathroom.

I had to think quick. Cover yourself, I thought. So I grabbed the shower curtain, tore it off the hooks, and wrapped it around myself.

That helped, but the hot water was still jetting from everywhere and the plastic shower curtain felt like it was going to melt on my back.

I dodged the worst streams but wherever I moved in the tiny bathroom a forceful jet of water seemed to seek me out, piercing me with hot needles.

I pulled again on the door. The doorknob came off in my hands. I stood staring at it like a total moron, feeling the metal grow hot in my numb fingers.

Meanwhile the water was getting hotter and hotter. As hot as boiling water. Hot enough to steam me alive.

11

I tried to get a grip on the door with my slipping fingernails, squirming to avoid the worst of the water's fury.

In another few seconds I'd be boiled like a lobster.

A sudden rush of cool air seemed like a dream. "Jason!"

No dream. My mother's hand closed on my arm, pulling me out into the hall, away from the scalding water. I was saved.

"The house wants to get me, Mom!" I blurted out. "It wants to kill me!"

"Hush now, let me help," Mom said. "Let's see how bad it is."

She helped me take off my hot, wet T-shirt and checked my back for burns. Luckily the shower curtain had done a pretty good job protecting me.

"That was a close call," she said, and kissed me on the forehead like she did when I was little. Usually I hate that, but I didn't this time.

Just then Dad came in the front door. His whistle died on his lips when he saw the steam boiling from the bathroom.

"Dave!" Mom said. "Jason almost got badly burned!"

"It's that old plumbing," Dad said, rolling up his sleeves. "I'll check it out."

My skin felt tender, especially on the back of my neck, but once I was cooled off and in dry clothes I was hungrier than ever.

I was just mopping up the last of the maple syrup when Dad came into the kitchen, drying his hands and looking pleased, like he always did when tackling a new project.

"Those pipes were about rusted through," he said to me. "Just your bad luck to be there when they decided to blow."

Dad turned to Mom, who still looked a little pale from the incident. "We'll have to watch out for things like that," he said cheerfully. "This is an old house. I expect there's lots of things ready to give way as soon as we lay hands on them. But we knew that when we rented the place, right?"

Mom looked at me. "Jay seems to think the house is out to get him."

Dad said, "It was just an accident, Jay. It could have happened to any one of us."

"Forget it," I said.

Maybe the crazy laughter had really been the steaming, rattling pipes. I didn't really think so, but there was no way my parents were going to believe me, and I wasn't in the mood for a lecture on my overactive imagination.

Still, it *did* seem like something was out to get me. How come all the "accidents" in the house seemed to be happening to me? And how come my mother could open the bathroom door so easily when I'd pulled and tugged with all my might, just to have the doorknob come off?

A guy could get paranoid around here, that was for sure! But before I had a chance to really brood on it, Steve knocked on the backdoor and shouted my name.

He was standing out there with a bat over his shoulder. "Game time," he said. "I know you can catch, let's see if you can hit."

Excellent! That would get my mind off this crazy house. I ran upstairs to get my ball and glove. I was heading for the stairs, thinking about maybe sliding down the banister, when I froze. It was like sparkles of ice suddenly forming in my veins.

Strange laughter.

I listened and there it was again. Echoing in the hallway. And it seemed to be coming from Sally's room.

Very quietly I tiptoed down the hall and stopped outside her door. Inside, Sally giggled — and there was another, answering laugh. A child's laughter. But not Sally. Definitely not Sally.

I put my hand on the doorknob. It was icy to the touch, so cold my fingers almost stuck, frozen in place. I got a grip on the baseball, ready to throw it with all my might, and leaned my shoulder into the door.

It popped open and suddenly I was inside.

Sally was sitting on the floor, playing by herself. She didn't seem the slightest bit afraid, and she was smiling at the space across from her, as if someone was there. But she was alone, completely alone.

And then I saw her pick up Winky, her favorite stuffed bunny, and hold it out, almost as if she was giving it to someone, someone just her size. Of course, there was no one there. Nobody but me, watching.

Sally let go of the bunny.

It hung there, suspended in midair.

"NO!" I shouted.

The flop-eared animal fell to the floor.

Sally glared at me, her lower lip stuck out. "You scared him away," she complained.

"Who?"

Sally turned away, blond curls bouncing.

I went into the room and knelt beside her. "Who, Sally?" I asked gently. "Who did I scare away?"

"My new friend," she answered sulkily, refusing to look at me.

"What new friend?" I put an arm around her

51

and gave her a squeeze. "Come on, Sally, you can tell me."

She squirmed away. "Go away. You're mean."

I couldn't get another word out of her. Sally can be very stubborn, and when she gets in one of her moods she won't talk. I kept asking her questions about this invisible friend of hers and she kept shaking her head.

Finally I gave up and went downstairs. Steve was sitting in my chair, eating pancakes. He looked at me and grinned.

"Mom, I just saw something weird in Sally's room," I said, knowing it sounded lame. But I had to tell her, no matter how crazy it sounded. Sally might be in danger.

I described what happened with the bunny and what Sally had said about her new friend.

Steve looked at me bug-eyed but Mom just laughed. "Lots of kids Sally's age make up invisible playmates. It's perfectly healthy. She must have been holding that bunny somehow, Jay, and you just couldn't see it."

I wasn't exactly surprised when no one believed me about the bunny floating in midair. I could hardly believe it myself. So I decided to change the subject. "Did you come in and open my window last night?" I asked Mom. Maybe there was a rational explanation for that, too.

"No, of course not. We haven't got the screens up yet. Which reminds me. I'll have to get your father to look for them in the basement. She added a note to the list she was making.

"Well, someone opened it," I said. "And it sure wasn't me. And then it slammed down and almost took my head off. I was going to tell you about it at breakfast but then the bathroom decided to blow up and try to boil me alive."

Mom frowned with concern. "What you need is some fresh air, young man. Blow the cobwebs away." Her tone softened. "You had a frightening experience this morning, Jason. I don't blame you for feeling shaken up. You need to get it off your mind."

"I'll keep his mind off it, Mrs. Winter," Steve said. "He gets a load of my fastball, he won't be able to think of anything else."

My mother nodded happily. "Great. Go ahead, Jay. Go out and play with your new friend." She winked at Steve. "He's not imaginary, is he?"

12

We fooled around in the backyard for a while, with Steve pitching and me hitting, but with nobody else around to field the ball we got tired of chasing it down.

"Let's check out the lake," Steve suggested.

There was a boat landing and a recreation area on the lake, but there wasn't much of anybody around yet, so we ended up skipping stones.

Steve made it look easy. He'd take this small rock and cock it in his fingers and then flick his wrist and the stone would skip across the water like something alive.

When I tried it, the stones kept going plop! and sinking right away.

"Like this," said Steve, showing me how to flick my wrist.

I tried again and was amazed to get three skips.

But Steve shook his head. "Your stones are too round," he said. "You need flat ones and you have to hold them like this."

"Yeah, okay," I said, and started searching around the shore for flat rocks.

"I've been skipping stones since I was about three years old," Steve said, showing me how to position my thumb and forefinger. "I'm surprised the lake's not filled in by now."

Once I got into the rhythm of it, I learned pretty quickly. And concentrating almost made me forget about the old house and the evil laughter and the bursting pipes and the invisible playmates.

I reared back and skipped a stone that seemed to bounce clear across the lake.

"Oh, no," Steve cried. "What have I done? I've created a monster!"

"Dr. Frankenstein!" I said, making a monster face.

We fooled around some more and I was surprised at how fast the time flew by.

On the way back up Cherry Street we looked up and saw the house, or what you could see of it peeking through the tall trees. It was cool in the shade and I shivered in my damp T-shirt.

Steve got this serious look on his face. "All that stuff you said about the house," he said slowly. "Was it true?"

I shrugged. I wanted to make some joke and laugh it off but it was like the house might be listening. Overhead the pine branches scraping against each other made whispery sounds.

" 'Cause I'm not sure whether I should tell you

this," said Steve. He glanced away, like he was afraid to look me in the eye.

"Tell me," I demanded, grabbing Steve's arm.

"OK, OK," said Steve. "But you have to promise not to tell anyone."

I nodded impatiently. "I promise."

Steve leaned close to me and squinted up at the house. He lowered his voice almost to a whisper. "This happened a few years ago when I was just a little kid and didn't know what to do about anything."

I nodded. "Go on."

"I wandered over here to check the old place out, right? I was right by that tree with the flowers by the side of the house — "

"It's a cherry tree," I said.

"Whatever," said Steve, glaring at me. "I just happened to look up." He paused and bit his lip as if remembering something he hoped to forget.

"Come on," I said. "Tell me."

Steve sighed deeply. "I looked up and saw this old lady in the kitchen tying something up. It looked funny — kind of wiggly — so I crawled closer until I was right under the window. Then I stood and looked in." Steve's eyes widened. "You're not going to believe what I saw."

I groaned. "Probably not."

"You know, it's not easy for me to tell you about this," said Steve, acting as if his feelings were hurt.

"All right. I won't say another word," I promised.

"There was a little kid in there," whispered Steve. "She'd squeezed him into a roasting pan and while I was watching she stuck him in the oven and cooked him just like you cook a turkey!"

Suddenly Steve pushed me and burst out laughing. "You believed me!" Steve hooted.

"No way, you liar."

"You should have seen your face." He made a bug-eyed face with his mouth hanging open, drool spilling out the side.

I winced, but Steve was laughing too hard to keep it up for long.

"*Jayyy-sonnnnn!*"

That was Mom, calling me for lunch.

"See you later, you liar," I said.

Steve stopped me. He looked serious again, as if he was sorry for making stuff up. I should have known better.

"Better take a close look at your lunch, Jason," he teased. "Better check that your mom's not feeding you roasted little kid!"

13

Sally was eating peanut butter and jelly. Mom was at the stove, frying something that smelled like hamburger. "Wash your hands," she said automatically.

"But, Mom — " I thought she should cut me a little slack after my morning washing experience.

"The pipes are fixed," she interrupted. "I think it's safe to go back in the bathroom."

No point in arguing. Sally giggled as I left the kitchen and went into the bathroom.

Here goes nothing, I thought, and approached the sink warily. The new pipes gleamed. I left the door open and twisted the faucet lever slowly, ready to get out of there in a hurry. But the water flowed normally and there were no strange noises in the plumbing.

At least *that* was fixed.

When I went back into the kitchen there was a bun on my plate. I picked up the top, checked it out. Looked like hamburger. I glopped ketchup on it and took a big bite. Yep, tasted like hamburger.

"When you finish your lunch, Jay, check the basement and see if there are any extra trash cans," said Mom, wiping Sally's face and hands. "Your father has promised to take Sally for a walk while I get some work done in the office. So I want it quiet around here, OK?"

"No problem, Mom," I said, and made a zipping motion across my lips.

I wolfed down the rest of the burger, trying to think how I'd get back at Steve for that stupid story. It would have to be something really good. Lock him in the attic for a couple of hours, maybe.

I was on my way up to my bedroom to change for a swim when I remembered about the trash cans. Right. Check out the basement.

The basement door was off the kitchen. I hadn't been down there yet. I wondered if anyone had. Maybe my dad, looking for screens. Or maybe not, he'd been pretty busy setting up the office.

Go on, get it over with. What's the big deal?

I opened the basement door and peered down into the dark. The air coming up out of the basement was cold and dank. There was a light switch by the door. I flipped it on and was relieved to see the stairs spring into view all the way to the shadowy bottom.

The steps were old and worn, rounded at the edge of each tread. I started down. The stairs creaked loudly. The musty smell grew stronger and the air colder.

I couldn't find another light switch at the bottom of the stairs. There was only the one bare bulb hanging on a wire from the ceiling, and it was pretty dim. It didn't look as if anybody had been down here in years. Cobwebs hung off the light-bulb.

I stood at the bottom of the stairs and looked around. The basement was big and it was full of old boxes and things that cast strange shadows.

Way in the back I spotted something that looked like a trash can.

My nerves were on edge, but there was nothing to be scared of, right? Right? So I worked my way over to where I'd seen the trash can. Or something that looked like a trash can. What else could it be?

A long snaky shadow reared up at me. I jumped, but it turned out to be a floor lamp.

The next step my foot sank into something soft. I jumped back and kicked at it. An old pillow.

The farther I got from the safety of the stairs — and the small pool of light from the single bulb — the more it felt as if I was entering another world. A world full of small, secret, furtive sounds and creatures hidden beyond the reach of my eyes. A world that thrived in the shadows and in years of layers of dust.

I let out my breath when I got to the trash can.

I didn't belong down here with all these creepoid shadows and I was going to leave, right now.

I picked up the trash can. And it started to shake.

A thumping, drumming noise started up — inside the can!

I tried to let go, but my hands were stuck to the handles. I went nuts trying to get loose, and finally the can fell with a clang, tipping onto its side.

A tiny, terrified mouse escaped, running for its life. Just a mouse!

I slumped in relief. Then I wiped my sticky hands on my shorts and picked the trash can up again, peeking cautiously inside. Empty. The startled mouse must have been flinging itself around in blind panic. It made a lot of noise for such a little thing — must have been amplified by the metal sides of the can. Yeah, that was it.

Scared by a stupid little mouse — good thing Steve wasn't here to see that.

I dragged the can back across the floor, making enough noise to drown out any other scuttling mice. It felt safer when I reached the circle of light. At the bottom of the stairs I looked up.

For some reason the stairway looked longer from down here. Maybe because of the dim light. Some kind of optical illusion. Whatever, I was heading back up right that very minute, anxious to return to the daylight.

As I heaved the can up the stairs, the shadows seemed to be pulling me backwards, as if they wanted me to stay down there in the dark.

Was that the shadows sighing?

I paused, holding stock-still. Something was making a sighing noise. What was it?

I heard breathing. Ragged breathing

Something coughed.

It was right under me. There was somebody hiding under the stairs!

I started to run up the stairs.

But I didn't get far.

An icy hand reached up between the treads and snagged my ankle.

Bony fingers gripped me like iron.

Then I heard a soft, triumphant cackle beneath the stairs.

14

I yelled.
 I screamed and kicked and pulled, but the thing held on.

My heart sank when I remembered no one could hear me. Dad and Sally were outside and Mom was in the office with the door closed.

It had me and it wouldn't let go.

The icy grip was burning into my flesh, eating through to the bone. It was too dark to see, but in my imagination I pictured a fleshless creature under the stairs, scaly, sharp-toothed mouth grinning at me.

Got to get loose!

I kicked harder. I had to get away, but whatever had my ankle wouldn't let go. I couldn't see anything down there, but something told me there was a second claw ready to snatch my other ankle. Once it had both feet, I was a goner.

I strained until it seemed as if my muscles would snap like rubber bands. Then with a crack and a sudden jolt the step gave way, the tread breaking through.

There was a scream from under the stairs and the bony claw let go of my ankle.

I yanked my foot free and scrambled up the stairs on my hands and knees.

I slammed the door and leaned against it, my chest heaving.

When I finally got my breath back I looked down at my hands and almost laughed. I still had the trash can!

Good going, butter brains, you're a real hero. Except the only reason you didn't let go is because you were too scared to think straight.

I dragged the trash can outside and left it there, prying my hands off the sticky handles.

"Hey, Jay!"

My dad was shouting from the top of the hill, where he and Sally were playing. I waved. Then I ran up to them, ready to tell Dad about what had happened in the basement.

With every step I became less sure. What really *had* happened?

The dim basement had gotten on my nerves. A little mouse had scared me. My ankle had gotten caught between the steps.

And the laugh? Maybe that evil laughter was all in my head.

When I got up to the top of the hill the first

thing I said was, "Better not go down into the basement, Dad."

"Oh? Why is that?"

"The steps got busted. They're pretty old and rotten, I guess."

"Thanks for the warning," he said. He glanced at my ankle. "I notice you're limping, are you OK?"

"Yeah, I'll be fine. Just make sure you don't go down there, OK? You or anybody else."

Dad looked at me kind of funny. "Sure, anything you say," he said. "Your new friend Steve was around — wanted to know if you wanted to go swimming. Said he'd meet you down at the lake."

Steve. I'd almost forgotten.

Ten minutes later I was cannonballing off the end of the dock. KERPLUNK! The water was cold but it felt good. It woke me up, as if the incident in the basement had been some kind of bad dream.

Except my ankle was still sore. So that part was true.

I figured it was partly Steve's fault, telling me that spooky story. Putting ideas into my head. So I decided to get back at him. It turned out he didn't like to touch bottom in the lake.

"Gross," he said. "The mud squishes between your toes."

"What are you afraid of, Steve?"

"I just think it's gross, that's all," he said.

But he was real jumpy in the water, like he was scared something was going to bite him. Snapping turtles or snakes. I'm a pretty good swimmer — better than Steve, as it turned out — and that gave me an idea.

When Steve wasn't looking, I dove under as quietly as I could and swam in his direction. I reached down, got hold of his big toe, and held on.

Even under water I could hear him yelling bloody murder.

"Help!" he screamed. "Help! It's got me! Help!"

It was great. I held on as long as I could and then let go and broke the surface with a huge splash. I was laughing so hard I had to get out of the water. Steve was beet red.

"Gotcha," I said.

"That's cheating. I never snuck up on you. All I did was tell a scary story."

"Hey, Steve!"

I wheeled around. That was a girl's voice calling Steve. It turned out to be this black-haired girl with big, dark eyes. She came down to the landing and stood there with her hands in the pockets of her denim cutoffs. "I heard somebody calling for help," she said.

"Forget about it, Lucy," Steve said. He made a face at me to shut up.

"Hi," I said. "We were just fooling around." I

stuck out my hand. "I'm Jason. Do you live around here, Lucy?"

"My family comes here every summer," she said, smiling. "I've known Steve since I was six."

"Careful of him, Lucy." Steve warned. "Jason's our age but sometimes he acts about six. Or maybe he's possessed by the old witch that haunts that house he's staying in."

"Whaaat?" Lucy raised her eyebrows at me.

"Steve's just mad 'cause he can't take a joke," I said.

"Jason's spending the summer in that creepy old place on Cherry Street," said Steve. "The one that weird old lady used to live in."

Lucy's eyes widened. "I've heard stories about that place, too. What's it like, living there?"

"What kind of stories?" I asked, my pulse quickening.

Lucy looked away. "Nothing much really. Just silly stuff. You know how people make things up."

"Go on, Lucy," urged Steve wickedly. "Tell him."

"Yeah," I said. "Tell me." At first I didn't want to know but now I had to, she was acting so mysterious.

"Well," said Lucy. "A family came to stay in that house last year but they only stayed a couple of days."

I nodded. Steve had already told me that.

"My parents talked to them just before they

left. They said that one night the ghost of an old woman came into their kids' bedroom," said Lucy. "Although it wasn't an old woman, really, more a skeleton, all bent over and wearing some kind of black cape. She pointed her fingerbone at the little kids and warned them to get out. They said her voice sounded like it came from the grave."

I snorted. It sounded like another made-up story.

Lucy held up her hand. "That's not the end of it. The ghost then snapped her skeleton fingers and there was a huge clap of thunder and the bed lifted up and turned over on the kids. They thought they were going to suffocate! Their parents found them like that, trapped under the bed. Naturally they left the next day and nobody's been in that house since. Until you." She looked questioningly at me.

I tried to think of something funny to say but nothing sprang to mind. "There's always stories about old houses," I finally said dismissively.

"Of course," said Lucy. "We know there isn't really any such thing as ghosts."

She had a real nice way of laughing, I noticed.

Lucy took a band off her wrist and pulled her long hair into a ponytail. "The real truth is probably something boring like the kids heard noises all night. All old houses make strange noises. They got scared and made up that story so their parents would leave."

"Or maybe she threatened to roast the kids like Thanksgiving turkeys," Steve said with a big laugh, shoving me and then dodging away.

"Or maybe she sneaked in and pinched their toes, scaring them half to death," I teased.

Lucy looked at us and shrugged. "I don't know what you're talking about, but I'm going for a swim."

"I'll come, too," I said.

"I'm waterlogged," said Steve, dropping into one of the wooden chairs on the little beach.

As we entered the water, I turned to Lucy and asked what she knew about the house on Cherry Street. "Okay, you don't believe in ghosts," I said. "But was there really an old lady who lived there?"

Lucy nodded, her eyes very serious. "Oh, yes. For years and years. She was kind of crazy, I guess. If a kid so much as stepped on her property she would come out screaming and cursing them. Everybody said she was a witch. But that was a long time ago. I don't remember her at all. She died when I was a little girl."

I took a deep breath. I had to know. "Did she die in the house?"

Lucy hesitated. "No one really knows. They never found her body."

15

When I pushed open the door to my bedroom I was thinking pretty hard about what Lucy had told me about the old lady.

Then I stepped inside and my heart went right up into my throat.

The room was in chaos. It looked as if a monster had torn it apart with his bare hands. Stuff I hadn't bothered unpacking was thrown all around. Models I'd left in the boxes were all in pieces, scattered everywhere. My clothes were tied up in knots and draped around, hanging from the bedposts.

Worse, the pillow feathers were everywhere. It looked like a million chickens had been fighting on my bed. The mattress was hidden under a layer of tiny white feathers.

What had really happened here? Who had done this?

I approached the bed cautiously. My pillow had

been cut to ribbons and the feathers thrown every which way.

Then I noticed it. Something metal sticking out of the mattress. Slowly I reached out and brushed away feathers.

I jerked my hand away as if I'd been burned.

Mom's super-sharp cutting shears. They were plunged up to the hilt in my mattress — right in the spot my heart would be if I had been sleeping!

I yanked the shears out of the mattress and looked around in a panic. I remembered what Lucy had said — "The kids probably made up the whole story to get their parents to leave." That's what my parents would think if they saw this mess. That I'd done it myself to prove that weird things started happening the minute we moved into this creepy old house.

Think quick, butter brains. You've got to clean this mess up before they see it. And you'll have to sneak those shears back into the office without getting caught.

First thing, I found a pillowcase and stuffed as many of the loose feathers into it as I could. They were hard to grab and it took forever, but finally the room looked as if only two or three chickens had been fighting, not a million like before.

Next I put the toys and models away, and un-knotted my clothes, and put everything back where it was supposed to be. I found another pillow in the closet and hid the one that had been cut up.

All the time I was wondering if maybe Steve had snuck up and done this just to scare me. Was that his idea of a practical joke? Was he just getting even with me for giving him a scare at the lake?

I was going to find out first thing tomorrow, first thing.

Getting the shears back into the office turned out to be not so hard. I put them in an empty shoe box and carried the box downstairs as if I didn't have a care in the world. If anybody asked, I'd say it was my baseball card collection, and everybody was so sick of me making them look at the cards they'd never want to see what was inside the box.

Downstairs I waited until Mom and Dad were both in the kitchen, and then I ducked into the office and closed the door softly.

It was dark in the room and I didn't dare turn on the lamp. Enough light came in the windows from the night sky so I could find my way around. Dad had set up his drafting table, and there were blueprints unfurled on just about every flat surface. Mom's computer was on the desk — you could see the little green warm-up light. All the drafting tools were laid out on the worktable, right where the cutting shears should have been.

I had just put the shears back in place when the lamp snapped on.

"Jay? Looking for something?"

It was my father. He was standing in the doorway, staring at me.

"I, ah, need some rubber bands," I said. "For my card collection."

I held up the shoe box.

"How were you going to find them in the dark?" Dad asked.

"I couldn't find the light switch."

Dad looked at the shoe box and then at me, and he sort of smiled. Like he didn't want to know exactly what I was up to.

"Here," Dad said, handing me a package of rubber bands. "That's enough for ten card collections."

"Thanks, Dad," I said.

I was sweating like a pig from relief. Whew! That was a close one. I decided to get back up to my bedroom and make sure all the feathers were cleaned up.

I was passing by Sally's room when I heard her chatting happily.

It sounded like she was talking to someone, but hers was the only voice.

A chill went through me.

I stopped and put my ear to the door. There were pauses as if she was listening and then giggles as if what the other person said was funny.

I tried to shake off the eerie tingle that crept up my spine.

Sally often talked to her dolls, I reminded myself. It sounded just the same. Well, almost the same.

I opened the door as quietly as I could.

Sally was sitting on the floor in front of a coloring book. As I watched, she selected a crayon, held it out, then returned it to the box.

Sally glanced up and smiled when she saw me. "Bobby doesn't like red," she said matter-of-factly.

"Oh, really," I said, stepping into the room. There was a second coloring book, I noticed, set out beside Sally's.

"Is that Bobby's book?" I asked.

Sally nodded, blond curls bobbing. "He's a good colorer, isn't he? And he's never even seen a coloring book before today or even a crayon." Sally giggled as if this was amazing, more amazing than her friend's invisibility.

I leaned over to look at the two books — and caught my breath in shock.

Sally's book looked like her pictures always did — wide swatches of color, none too careful about the lines. The other book showed very careful, short strokes neatly inside the lines.

Someone else had been there, coloring in her book.

16

I snatched up the two coloring books and ran downstairs. Dad was in the living room, reading a magazine. I put the coloring books down on the coffee table and stood back and said, "Look!"

Dad raised his eyes at me. "Some of your handiwork?" he joked.

"Look at them," I insisted. "They were done by two different kids!"

Dad looked from one to the other. He nodded. "One's very controlled, subdued colors. And this one — obviously Sally's usual wild flamboyance. Very interesting."

"Then you believe me?"

"Believe you?" Dad looked puzzled. "It's not a matter of believing anything, Jason. I can see they're different. Obviously, Sally's imaginary friend is so important to her she's devised a way to make him seem real by coloring in a style that's almost opposite her own inclinations." Dad rose

75

from his chair. "I've got to show these to your mother. Amazing."

I gritted my teeth and pounded my fist on the back of the now-empty chair. What would it take to make them believe me?

But wait. Why should they believe me?

What if I was wrong and they were right? My father's explanation made perfect sense. And I hadn't actually seen a crayon moving through the air by itself, had I?

But what about this morning, when I'd seen the bunny hanging in midair?

What if my eyes were playing tricks on me? Maybe Sally really had been holding the stuffed animal up somehow, pretending she was giving it to Bobby.

But what about the bursting pipes? Was it so strange that old pipes would break?

And what about all the strange noises in the middle of the night? That eerie voice calling my name? Maybe there was a rational explanation for that, too, just like the incident in the basement had been an accident — my foot breaking through a slimy old stair, making me think there was a bony hand grabbing my ankle.

As for the shears stabbed into my mattress, that had to be Steve. Definitely Steve.

"Jason?" Mom called from the kitchen. "Your friend Steve is here."

That proved it. He'd come back to see how

scared I was. So I decided to play it cool, not let on that I knew.

"Hey, Steve." I slapped him five.

"I don't want you boys going far," Mom said.

"We'll be on the porch," I said. "Just fooling around, right, Steve?"

"I guess so," he said uncertainly.

When we were out on the porch, Steve took a bag out of his pocket and put it on the table. He had a chocolate chip cookie in his hand and he munched it. "My Mom made these. Help yourself."

"No, thanks," I said.

"You don't like cookies?" he said, sounding disappointed.

"I like cookies fine, but first I want to settle something."

"Sure," he said, eyeing the bag. "What's up?"

"Swear on your mother's grave you'll tell the truth?"

Steve made a face as he finished his cookie. "You think I'm a liar, is that it?"

"Just say you'll swear."

"OK, fine. I swear on my mother's grave I'll tell the truth. Satisfied?"

"Almost," I said. "Now tell me about the shears."

"What?"

"The shears you took out of my parents' office and stabbed into my mattress."

Steve stood up. "You know what, Jason? You're totally out of your mind."

You could tell he was telling the truth.

"Take it easy," I said. "I believe you."

I told him what had happened.

"Maybe it was your little sister," he suggested.

"No way. She's not big enough. It was like something really strong just plain went nuts in my room. Like it hated me."

"You're scaring me, you know that, Jason?" Steve said, rolling his eyes. "Here, have a cookie before I eat them all up."

Steve handed me the bag. I put my hand in and felt for a cookie.

My hand closed on something squishy.

Something gross and slimy.

"Oh, no," shouted Steve. "Wait! I picked up the wrong bag. That's the dog poop I cleaned off the front walk!"

I dropped the bag and jumped away. And felt as if I was going to barf.

Steve exploded with laughter. He laughed so hard, he fell on the porch and rolled around. "Gotcha," he cried when he caught his breath. "Gotcha good. Now we're even."

I headed into the house.

"Hey, Jason, it's only rubber. Fake dog poop. I bought it at the joke shop." Steve laughed some more. "Jason, here's the real cookies. Don't you want one?"

He was still laughing when I went inside.

17

The aliens came bursting out of their hiding places in the hills, about to swarm down on the unsuspecting town and take over the minds of the townspeople. Thrilling and exciting and all that stuff — but I couldn't concentrate.

I turned a page and realized I'd read through half the battle without understanding a word. Something else was clamoring for attention.

I put the book down. What was it?

Sally. Her voice was drifting faintly down the hallway. She should be asleep by now. But she sounded as if she was comforting someone.

I strained my ears but I couldn't make out any words. Just the tone. A calming, soothing tone, as she sometimes used with her dolls.

Nothing weird about that, right? But my heart was starting to beat faster.

Then Sally's voice rose. "Nooo," she said.

I sat up and swung my feet to the floor. I didn't want to go down the hall. No way.

But I had to check on my kid sister.

She was probably having a bad dream, I told myself. I'd look in on her and then come back and finish my book.

I cracked open my bedroom door and shivered in the suddenly cold air.

I started to go through the door and something bounced me right back. I landed on my butt and stared up at the doorway in disbelief.

There was nothing there. Nothing to stop me from leaving. And yet it had.

I got up and slowly walked forward again.

SLAP! I was sproinged back into the room. This time I managed to keep my balance and not fall down. I approached the doorway more slowly, reaching out. My hand came up against an icy-cold barrier. It felt rubbery, like some kind of weird, invisible Jell-O. It yielded a little but I couldn't push through. And it felt completely creepy — clammy and slippery and unlike anything I'd ever felt before. Just touching it made the hairs stand up on the back of my neck.

"Jay-son!"

That was Sally, calling me. And I couldn't get out of my own bedroom. Something wanted to keep me from helping Sally!

I couldn't let that happen. I was getting through that icky stuff one way or another.

I got down in a three-point stance, tensed myself, and then charged full blast at the door. I sank to my waist in the invisible, icy goo. I started punching at it as hard as I could, desperate to get through.

The slimy, Jell-O-like stuff tightened around my head, slowed my fists until I couldn't move at all, forward or backwards. It seeped into my ears and nose, squeezing my head.

The invisible stuff was sucking me in, digesting me slowly, cell by cell. It felt as if my skin was dissolving.

It was eating me!

I opened my mouth to scream and the gelatinous mass swam over my tongue and flowed down my throat. I was suffocating.

I struggled and wriggled, pulled with all my might. My chest was burning with effort and lack of air. I heard pounding footsteps on the stairs — somebody was coming, but who?

Suddenly there was a loud sucking noise and the goo let go. I fell back on the floor with a crash. What breath I had left was knocked out of me.

As I lay there gasping like a fish, my dad appeared in the doorway. His face was white with shock and alarm.

"Jason! What happened? Are you all right?"

Mom's face appeared behind Dad's shoulder. She, too, was pale, her eyes wide.

"Sally," I croaked.

Mom dashed down the hall to Sally's room while Dad came in and helped me up. I blurted out everything that had happened, how the house seemed to be after me and Sally, and how the invisible goo had blocked the doorway and prevented me from helping her.

Dad went to the doorway and ran his hand up and down in the empty space. "There's nothing here, Jason," he said, his eyes troubled. He walked into the hall and then back into the room to demonstrate. "Nothing at all."

Mom came running back. "Sally's fine. She's sound asleep," she said, looking anxiously at me. "What's going on?"

Dad shook his head and picked up my book off the bed. "Apparently Jay had a nightmare," he said, showing the cover to Mom. It showed fighting monsters with blood that looked a lot like green Jell-O.

"You sure gave us a scare," said Mom, rearranging my covers."

I stopped shaking after a while. It was easier to let my parents believe I'd just had a vivid nightmare, but I knew it was no dream.

There was something evil in this house.

Something that was careful to hide itself from my parents.

Something that wanted me and Sally dead.

18

I woke up dreaming that something was screaming at me. It turned out to be a bird on the windowsill, cheeping and peeping like crazy.

Just what I needed, an alarm clock with wings.

But when I'd had a chance to shake the sleep out of my head, I decided the bird had the right idea. It was another great summer day and I didn't want to waste it.

The bright, golden sunshine made what had happened last night seem distant, like maybe it really had been a dream. I knew it wasn't, but I really didn't want to think about it. The daylight made everything seem OK.

No way was I going to let this stupid old house completely ruin my summer. There were too many cool things to do in the yard and around the lake. And so far the house hadn't really been able to hurt me — what was I so afraid of, anyhow? Ghosts couldn't hurt you unless you let them, everybody knew that.

I was nearly finished with my cornflakes when there was a knock at the kitchen door.

Steve. Time for payback.

I took a big gulp of orange juice and held it in my mouth as I flung open the door, ready to spray all over Mr. Plastic Dog Poop himself.

"Hi, Jason."

Oops. I hurriedly swallowed my orange juice. "Um, hi, Lucy," I gulped.

"Some kids are going to meet behind the school to play ball," said Lucy. She had on a lime-green baseball cap with her ponytail pulled through the back, and was dressed in cutoffs and a white T-shirt. "If you bring a lunch, we can picnic at the lake afterwards."

"No prob," I said, and slapped together a peanut butter sandwich.

Steve showed up just as we were leaving. He gave me a secret grin but he didn't mention the trick with the dog poop.

"How's it going, Jay? Get a good night's sleep?" he teased.

"What do you care?" I said.

Steve looked hurt. "Hey, I was only asking. All that weird stuff you told me about, I was worried."

Lucy gave us both a look. "I've been asking around about the house on Cherry Street," she said. "We'll talk about it after the game."

My heart lurched. "What have you found out?"

"Later," she said firmly, waving to some kids coming down the street.

The school with the softball diamond was only a few blocks away. Nothing I did could get Lucy to say more and in a couple of minutes the other kids joined us. I was so distracted I could hardly keep their names straight. What had Lucy found out about the house? Why did she look so grave?

At the ball field there wasn't time to worry. Lucy and Steve knew everybody, so they picked the teams. Steve ended up picking me for third base, which is the position I wanted. It's a lot better than getting stuck in right field and having to shag down all the balls that get hit out of bounds.

Me and my big mouth. Even with Steve pitching, third base turned out to be the hot spot. Some of those ground balls came at me at about a hundred miles an hour and it was all I could do to knock them down and make the throw to first.

I made a couple of stupid errors, but basically I did OK, and we ended up winning 15 to 13.

After the game we left the field and headed for the lake. I was kind of replaying the game in my head — especially the part where I knocked in two runs — and I'd almost forgotten that Lucy wanted to tell me something she'd learned about the house.

I was so out of it, I actually ate a couple of Steve's chocolate chip cookies. I was munching down when Lucy wrapped up her picnic stuff and said, "You haven't asked what I found out, Jason. Don't you want to know?"

I felt like a balloon getting deflated. All the good cheer went out of me. For a couple of hours it had been as if the house didn't exist.

"I hope it's not something too horrible," I said. But even as I spoke the sun went behind a cloud. That's how it felt — as if that house was a big cloud cast over my whole summer.

"No, not so horrible," said Lucy. "But I think maybe you do have a reason to worry. It turns out that a little boy who lived there years and years ago died there. He fell out of a tree. Or something like that. He's probably still haunting the place."

Steve made a farting noise. "Oh, yeah? What about the old lady? She lived there for about a hundred years and no ghost ever scared her away," he said.

"Yes, but the thing about child ghosts," said Lucy, "is that only other children can see them."

"My mom and dad sure can't see this one," I said. "But then again, neither can I."

"You can hear it, though," said Lucy. "You can feel its presence in the house."

"That's for sure," I said dejectedly. "And Sally can see it. I'm sure of that."

"That's what scares me," said Lucy, leaning forward. "What if the little boy ghost wants another child for company. Permanently."

I stared at her, my mind a wordless blank.

Even Steve looked horrified.

"Oh, my God," I said.

"I think you'd better keep an eye on her," Lucy said. "You're the only one who can keep her safe."

19

That night I pretended to be asleep when my parents came up to bed.

They couldn't help — it was up to me.

Once the house was quiet — as quiet as it ever got — I dragged the chair from my room out into the hall and down next to Sally's door, which was open just enough for me to see her bed.

I sat in the chair with a baseball bat across my knees, waiting. Let it come! I was pumped up. Nothing was going to hurt my little sister, not if I had anything to say about it.

Nothing happened. The house remained quiet. Sally slept peacefully. The hours slowly passed.

My eyes grew heavy. I fought to stay awake but it was no use. I drifted off listening to the slow, rhythmic sounds of Sally breathing gently as she slept. . . .

Suddenly I woke up with a start. At first I couldn't remember where I was, or what I was doing there. Then my mind cleared and my hands gripped the baseball bat.

A glance told me Sally's door was still open a few inches exactly as it had been. I was getting up to go inside and check on her when a noise from downstairs stopped me cold.

Screeeeek.

There was a scrape on the floor as if someone down there had bumped into a chair.

Eeeeeerk.

That was the sound of a drawer opening very slowly.

Steve. Maybe he was down there playing a prank after all that spooky talk.

Crouching close to the wall, I started hesitantly for the stairs, clutching the bat. More shuffling, stirring noises, then an eerie, echoey voice.

"Mama. My mama."

A child's voice! Sally must be down there!

I bolted down the stairs and tripped. Hanging on to the stair rail, I lost the bat. It was so loud thumping down the steps that surely it would wake my parents. And Steve would be scared off, right?

Right?

The noises stopped. I fumbled around for the light switch and clicked it on.

Nothing happened. The lights weren't working. It remained so dark I could barely see my own hands.

I heard a rustling noise. Cloth on cloth, some-body moving.

"Who's there?" I called out, my voice echoing in the darkness.

No answer.

I advanced slowly into the downstairs hall. A movement at my shoulder made me jump.

The clock. It was just the grandfather clock rearing up out of the dark, moonlight catching on its face. Just the clock — but my heart thudded.

"Sally?" I called softly.

No answer. I moved farther into the dining room.

Behind me a floorboard creaked. I whirled around. The shadows under the stairs stirred and parted. Cloth whispered against cloth.

If only I hadn't dropped the baseball bat.

"Dad?" I breathed, hopefully.

From under the stairs came a raspy, whispery voice. *"Where is it? You stole it from me, give it back!"*

My skin crawled. It was like the voice was get-ting inside me, making my blood freeze.

"Who — " My voice cracked. "Who's there?"

"NOOOOOOOOOOOOOO!"

Above me a child let out a piercing scream. It sounded as if it came from the top of the stairs. The scream seemed to free me and I tried to run up the steps.

Something hurtled out of the darkness. I

ducked and it whistled past my ear, just missing me.

"Ahhhh!"

Behind me, right behind me, there was a cry of pain as the object connected with something and bounced, striking an end table and knocking it over.

An antique lamp smashed to pieces.

I dropped to the floor, feeling around for the missing bat. My hand closed over something heavy and coldly metallic. I held it up. A bronzed baby shoe.

Something had hurled the heavy shoe at me — or maybe at something else on the stairs. Something behind me.

Then the shoe was torn from my grasp. Wham — it flew into the air and smashed into the chandelier, raining glass everywhere.

A piece of glass hit my leg and glanced off, cutting me slightly.

Got to get out of here! I stumbled for the stairs. The air seemed to crackle around my ears. My only thought was to reach my room. It wanted me, I had to get away!

Long, cold fingers came out of the shadows and snagged at my pajamas.

I jerked free and tried to run.

It was right behind me, gaining. Another whispery touch grazed my ankles.

Then I was at the top of the stairs, my room

only steps away. My breath wheezed in my chest. I reached for my bedroom door, threw it open and dived inside.

I flung myself against the door and held it closed. *Don't come in,* I prayed, *don't come in!*

Ghostly fingernails scraped along the door — *skreeeek, skreeeek* — and then moved on to rake the length of the wall.

On the other side of the door a hollow voice spoke right into my ear. *"I'll get you, Jason. You can't hide. I'll get you."*

Then the ghostly voice slowly faded and the house settled into silence as deep and soundless as the grave.

20

My skin was clammy and hot. When I opened my eyes the sun was beating down on me, already high. I had overslept, no surprise.

I dressed as fast as I could, eager to tell my parents what had happened last night. This time it would be different. They'd have to believe me, with all the damage downstairs. Finally they'd have to listen, they'd have to realize that both me and Sally were in danger. Like it or not we'd have to get out of this house.

Opening my door, I heard both Mom and Dad down in the kitchen. Good, I'd tackle them both at once.

Suddenly I felt a little uneasy. Why hadn't they come to wake me up when they found all that broken glass?

They were laughing down there in the kitchen. Weird. Very weird.

At the top of the stairs I stopped in surprise.

The bronzed baby shoe was back on its shelf.

Well, I realized, naturally Mom would have cleaned up the mess.

My jaw dropped in amazement as I started down the stairs. The chandelier was hanging in its place, completely undamaged!

I closed my eyes and opened them again. The chandelier was still there.

I went down a few more steps. There was the little end table. On it was the antique lamp that last night had been smashed to bits. It was untouched.

I picked it up and examined it. There wasn't so much as a crack.

What was going on here? Was I going crazy? Had it really all been a dream?

Then I looked down at my leg. There it was — the small cut where the chandelier glass had hit me, beaded with dried blood. It was no dream. It had really happened, just as I remembered it.

But Mom and Dad would never believe me. No point even telling them about it. Not until I had proof.

21

It was the bottom of the ninth, two out, with runners on second and third. I was holding down third base, keeping the runner on the bag. Our team was up by one run.

Just one more out and the game was ours.

"Hey, batter! Hey, batter!"

Steve pitched without a windup, holding the runners on. He threw a fastball right down the middle.

The batter swung and hit a soft ground ball right at me. An easy out. All I had to do was throw to home. No problemo.

I bent down to scoop up the ball and it went right through my legs.

Unbelievable. One runner crossed home plate, and before I could make a move, Lucy came around from second and passed me in a blur to score the winning run.

It was all my fault. After the game nobody said much. Steve just looked at me and shrugged.

I should have felt terrible, losing the game like that, but I didn't feel much of anything at all. A stupid baseball game, what did it matter?

"Hey, Jason, wait up!" It was Steve. "What happened to you? You looked like a zombie today. A real no-brainer."

"Thanks, Steve. You're a big help," I said. "If you'd had the kind of night I had, you'd still be hiding under your bed."

"Oh, yeah?" Steve's eyes lit up. "More ghost stuff, huh?"

"It's not funny," I said. "I'm really worried."

"Tell me," begged Steve. "I won't laugh. Maybe I can help. Two brains are better than one no-brainer."

Not that I expected him to believe me, but I told Steve everything that had happened. The noises, the things moving around downstairs, the voice outside my door. His eyes got bigger and bigger.

"When the chandelier smashed, a piece of flying glass hit my leg." I showed Steve the small cut. "I didn't get this in a dream. I keep looking for rational explanations but this time I have to admit, there aren't any. Broken lamps don't fly up and put themselves back together."

"Wow," said Steve, looking at the scratch. "So what do you think? Is it an old lady ghost or a little kid?"

I shrugged. "I don't know. Maybe there's two

of them. The voice was definitely not a child's. It sounded like a witch's voice. But I heard a little kid, too."

"Two ghosts? How come there'd be two ghosts haunting the same house?"

"I don't know," I said. "Maybe they're connected somehow."

"You mean like because of a murder or something? They say a ghost has to keep reliving the moment of its death. So if there's a little kid ghost, maybe he had something to do with the old lady dying!"

For some reason the very idea gave me the creeps. What if Steve was right? What if my little sister was playing with a ghost who had killed someone in real life?

Suddenly Steve turned in the road and slapped my arm. "I've got it," he said excitedly. "We can search for the old lady's body. The way to get rid of a ghost is to find the body and lay it to rest. Once the old lady's body is properly buried, maybe the child ghost will be at peace, too. Maybe that's what it wants, for you to find the body and get it out of the house."

It was a gruesome idea, searching for a body. But we had to try something.

"I'll bet it's in the basement," Steve said. "That's why nobody found it."

I didn't want to go down into that basement, not after what happened with the slimy hand grabbing my ankle, but Steve would think I was a chicken if I didn't. And besides, maybe I really had imagined that creepy hand.

So we did it, we went down into the basement.

My dad had fixed the broken step and the piece of wood was the only new and clean thing in the whole place.

I tensed when I put my foot down on the new step, listening for noises from under the stairs. But with Steve chattering away like a real motormouth, I couldn't hear a thing.

"Now I see why you brought that flashlight," said Steve. "It's pretty dim and spooky down here. The perfect place for a dead body."

We stopped within the circle of light from the overhead bulb and I switched on the flashlight. The flashlight beam turned hulking shadows into perfectly ordinary piles of junk — boxes, old tools, broken furniture.

We both stiffened when the door at the top of the stairs opened with a creak.

"Boys!" It was my mother. "Don't disturb those boxes in the corner," she said. "They belong to the owners of the house."

"OK, Mom," I called back. I aimed the flashlight at the other side of the basement. "We'll start there," I told Steve.

But Steve wouldn't make a move until I went first. It was much less scary down here when there were two of us, I decided. And thinking about it,

I didn't really expect to find anything, certainly not a forgotten skeleton, but exploring this creepy place with Steve would be cool.

"Blak!" Steve shouted suddenly, like he was choking.

I whirled around. The shadows moved in closer.

Steve was batting at his face and sputtering. "Spiderwebs! They're sticking to my face. Yuck!"

I laughed and the shadows retreated to their corners.

We found a bunch of moldering boxes filled with old magazines and newspapers, old-fashioned hats with net veils, unrecognizable parts of rusting metal.

"Look at these weirdos," Steve said, holding open an old magazine.

"That's how they dressed back then," I said.

"What a bunch of geeks."

"If you lived back then, that's how you'd dress, too," I pointed out.

"No way."

As it turned out, none of the boxes in that corner were big enough to hide a body.

We looked behind a ripped armchair that sprouted stuffing like fungus. Wrinkling my nose against the smell, I yanked the cushions off a sagging sofa while Steve held the flashlight over my shoulder.

No body. Not even a dead mouse.

Dust swirled as we shifted heavy boxes and

played the flashlight beam into corners that hadn't been disturbed in at least fifty years, maybe more.

"What's that?" cried Steve, tensing suddenly. "That noise."

I paused and listened. "I don't hear anything."

Steve suddenly grabbed my arm.

"There!" He pointed behind us, toward the corner where the owners' things were piled. "It sounds like someone moving around back there, trying to be quiet."

I listened. "Mice," I said, trying to keep the nervousness out of my voice. "I saw a mouse last time I was down here."

Steve looked doubtful. While we shifted around what seemed like millions of mildewed magazines, his gaze kept drifting toward that corner.

I could feel the darkness moving in closer each time my back was turned, like a game of red-light, green-light. Small noises nibbled at my attention but always stopped when I paused to listen.

When we found nothing more behind the stacks of magazines, Steve straightened up. Absently he wiped his filthy hands on his once-clean khaki shorts. "If there's a body down here, it's going to be over there," he said, gesturing toward the owners' piled belongings.

I nodded. "You're right. We'll just have to be careful to put things back so my mom doesn't get bent out of shape."

Very carefully and slowly we approached that

corner of the basement. It seemed darker there, as if the creepy shapes had a way of soaking up the beam from my flashlight.

"We can't move all this stuff," Steve complained. "It'll take forever."

"Hey," I said, with a tingle of excitement. "Is that a trunk?"

I pointed out a large rectangular shape standing on end behind a stack of boxes. "It's big enough to hold a body, isn't it?"

Immediately we both began heaving boxes out of the way until the trunk was clear. For a moment we just looked at it.

Then I reached slowly for the latch. I pulled. The lock clicked.

Nothing happened.

"My mom's calling," Steve said abruptly, taking a step backwards. "I've got to go."

"What? You can't leave now," I said, flabbergasted. "This could be what we've been looking for!"

"My mom will be mad," Steve said weakly, looking at the trunk reluctantly.

Faintly, I could hear Steve's mother in the distance. So he wasn't making that up.

"Just help me with this," I urged. I tugged again at the latch. "It's not locked, it's just stiff. If you hold the trunk steady I think I can get the lid open. It'll only take a minute."

Steve swallowed. "All right."

I grinned at him in the gloom and pried at the latch with both hands, grimly determined to get it open. I hadn't really believed we'd find a body down here, but now, faced with this body-sized trunk, my blood was humming. I just knew this trunk would help me solve the awful mystery of the house.

With a groan the rusted latch gave way. Eagerly I seized the lid and pulled it toward me like opening a door.

The lid creaked slowly open as if something feeble was trying to hold it closed from inside.

It was now or never, while Steve was still here. I yanked hard and the trunk came all the way open, creaking loudly in protest.

We both gasped.

There *was* a body.

As I stared, transfixed, it leaned out of the trunk and slowly, slowly toppled on top of me.

22

I raised my arms to fend the thing off. Gurgling noises came from my throat as I tried to fight free.

It was stiff and cold, a dead weight.

I flailed my arms and the thing rolled off me. I scrambled instantly to my feet, my chest heaving.

"A dressmaker's dummy!"

Weak with relief, Steve and I leaned against each other, laughing.

Then a small noise shut us up.

"Mice," I said automatically.

"Yeah," said Steve. "But, hey, I got to go before my mom kills me."

I nodded and picked up the flashlight from where it had fallen on the floor. "Steve, wait! There's something else in the trunk."

But Steve was already halfway up the stairs. "Later, Jason," he called over his shoulder.

I hesitated, then crouched down to reach into the trunk. It was quite deep and I had to crawl forward. My hand touched paper — a packet of envelopes tied with ribbon. I trained the flashlight on the packet and saw faded, spidery writing. Old letters!

Maybe this was a clue about what had happened in the house. Who had died here. Maybe even who had been murdered here.

Eager to find out, I put the flashlight on the floor and started to untie the ribbon right there. I was in such a hurry that my fingers fumbled with the knot and the packet dropped back into the trunk.

As I leaned over to get the package of letters back something slammed me hard in the back.

I lost my balance and tumbled headfirst into the trunk.

The lid slammed shut! The darkness was total. The space was so small I couldn't move, couldn't even shift around to push the lid with my feet.

As I thrashed weakly against the sides, I heard soft cackling laughter. Bony fingers scratched teasingly against the sides and lid of the trunk, sending shivers through my body.

I opened my mouth to scream but my chest was so tight nothing came out. In horror, I realized that there wasn't enough air. I was going to suffocate in here!

Then there really would be a body to find. Mine.

Frantically I rocked back and forth. Maybe I

could knock the trunk over, crack it open on the floor.

After what seemed an eternity of struggling, I felt the trunk slowly tilt, then fall with a thud. The lid popped open on impact, spilling me out onto the dirt floor.

I was on my feet in a flash.

But what about the letters? I had to get them. They could be the key to the whole thing.

I grabbed my flashlight and searched inside the trunk, trying to ignore the tingle of fear between my shoulder blades.

No letters. But they had to be here. I searched again, every inch, then forced myself to look under the trunk and all around the area. Nothing.

They were gone. They couldn't be, but they were. Whatever shut me inside must have gotten them.

My blood froze as I heard a slithering noise behind me. Then a cackle of laughter.

I bolted for the stairs. Nothing stopped me.

At the top I slammed the basement door and shot the bolt.

If there was a body down there, it could stay where it was!

23

Mom was in her office, making notes on some broad sheets of blue paper. As I went in she put down her ruler and looked at me, pencil in hand. She started to smile and then said, "Is that dirt all over your face? You look like a coal miner. What have you boys been up to?"

I shrugged. She'd never believe me about the trunk. I wasn't sure I believed it myself. "Oh, just exploring. There's a lot of neat old magazines down there."

"That's nice," said Mom, picking up her ruler and bending over her papers. "Go wash up, we'll be having dinner soon."

"Where's Sally?" I asked, turning to go.

"Napping," said Mom. She looked at her watch. "I'd better get her up or she'll never sleep tonight."

"I'll do it," I said, heading for the stairs.

"Wash up first," Mom called after me.

As soon as I reached the bottom of the staircase,

I started feeling anxious about Sally. Some kind of intuition told me something was wrong.

I took the stairs two at a time. The upstairs hall was completely silent. As if the house was holding its breath, just waiting for something to happen.

Sally's door was closed. She never had her door closed — she liked it open just the right number of inches.

I flung open the door. Sally — or something — was curled up under the bedclothes. "Sally?" I called quietly, tiptoeing over to the bed.

No answer. Slowly I pulled the blanket back. My stomach shuddered. No Sally. Someone had stuffed a pillow under the covers to make it look as if Sally was sleeping there. But Sally was gone.

As I raised my head, wondering what to do next, a gust of wind hit me full in the face. The window! It was open, with the screen removed and propped on the floor.

I ran to the window and stuck my head out.

"Hi, Jason!" Sally waved at me from the cherry tree below her window.

She was perched on a high branch. High enough so a fall might be fatal.

For a couple of heartbeats I couldn't think what to do. "Hold on tight," I said in a strangled voice, seeing that Sally was wobbling on her narrow branch, her other arm wrapped around her bunny. "I'll be right there to get you down."

But how? I swung my leg over the windowsill. But the uppermost branches of the tree looked too slender to take my weight. I stretched my leg out as far as it would go and my foot barely touched the end of a branch.

There was only one way. I'd have to climb up from below and grab her. But that meant leaving Sally alone while I ran back through the house.

"Hold on tight," I called down. "Don't move!"

Sally smiled at me and swung her feet.

I shuddered. She was so high up. If she fell she'd break her neck. "Don't move, Sally, please," I called again.

Then I ducked back inside and ran for the stairs. As I flew by the office I heard my mom ask what was going on.

"It's Sally," I shouted without stopping. "She's in the cherry tree."

Reaching the base of the tree, I looked up. Sally was impossibly high. She looked down at me and waved.

That threw off her balance.

My heart went into my throat. She was going to fall! She teetered, eyes going wide, mouth forming a little round "O" of fright. Then she managed to grab the trunk of the tree.

For the first time Sally seemed to realize she was in danger. She began to whimper.

"I'll get you down," I promised, hoisting myself up the tree trunk. "Just hold on."

The first few feet up were easy. Then the branches became thinner and grew so close together there was hardly room to move. My foot skidded on the smooth bark, and twigs whipped my face. I started slipping back.

Finally I managed to get a grip and pull myself up.

"Jason, what if I fall? Will you catch me?"

"Sally, don't fall. Just don't, OK?"

A branch, hardly more than a twig, snapped off under my foot. I had to hug the tree trunk to keep from falling. Slowly I managed to get back up.

Sally was still out of reach. I found another narrow wedge for my foot and got up a little higher. I was almost there. The branches bent and groaned under my weight.

I heard startled cries from below. My mother.

"Mom! See if you can find a ladder!"

"OK!" she yelled back. "Don't go any farther. That limb's not strong enough to support you both."

But Sally was too scared to act sensible. She started to cry as she reached out for my hand.

"No, Sally, stay there!"

But she wasn't listening. She stretched out her arm, impossibly far, and leaned forward, trying to reach me. She slipped, losing her balance.

I could only watch in horror as she fell.

At first she dropped quickly, and I almost closed my eyes. I couldn't bear to watch.

And then a strange thing happened. One moment she was hurtling down, and the next she seemed almost to float. As if something was holding her back.

"Jason! Jason!"

My little sister was floating just beyond my reach. Turning in the air to stretch her arms out at me. I grabbed for Sally's hand, missed, reached again, and clasped it.

Slowly she drifted gently down to nestle against my chest. And she was still holding her bunny!

I had my sister, but I was slipping. And with both hands full holding her, I couldn't get a grip.

"Jason, I'm here," cried Mom, leaning the ladder up against the tree trunk. "If I climb up can you hand Sally to me?"

"I think so." I didn't want to let go of Sally, not even to hand her to Mom. But I knew that would be safest. I might drop her trying to get her down myself.

I waited for Mom to get to the top of the ladder then crouched down to be as close as possible when I passed Sally to her.

It went off without a hitch, and once Mom and Sally were on the ground, I followed.

"How did she get up there?" Mom asked.

"Jason catched me," said Sally, beaming at me. "He catched me when I was flying."

Mom's face paled. "She started to fall?"

"It was the weirdest thing. It was like time

slowed down and held her up until I could grab her."

Mom hugged Sally tight. "That happens sometimes in a real emergency. Time seems to slow down and we seem to speed up."

"Maybe," I said skeptically. "But how did she get into the tree? When I checked on her, her window was open, and the screen was on the floor. But the tree is so far from her window, even I couldn't climb into it."

Sally twisted in Mom's arms. Her eyes were as clear as blue pools. "Bobby flied me to the tree," she said. "It's his favorite place. Me and Bobby and Winky like the tree."

Her invisible friend again. He'd almost killed her this time — or was it Bobby who had saved her?

"Little children have amazing dexterity," said Mom, shaking her head as she looked up at the tree. "We'll probably never know how she managed it. I'll have to remember to keep her window locked."

"I flied, Mommy," said Sally. "Bobby helped me to fly to Jason."

"Sure you did, honey. But I don't ever want you going up in that tree again. It's too dangerous."

Mom rose, carrying Sally.

"I flied! I flied!" Sally said, giggling as Mom carried her into the house.

Maybe I was crazy, but I believed her. Something had "flied" her to the tree. And something had saved her from falling. Maybe it was her invisible friend, the one she called Bobby.

But what kind of friend would put a little girl's life in danger in the first place?

Unless, of course, it wanted to make her into a ghost.

24

The next week went by without anything much happening. It was as if the house had gone to sleep, or given up and accepted us.

My parents spent most of their time in the office, poring over the blueprints, or on the telephone with the contractors who were going to build the new town complex. They were so busy with the project they hardly noticed when I offered to take Sally with me wherever I went.

Because I wasn't going to let it get my little sister.

Steve and Lucy were pretty understanding. They let me drag Sally around with us and they didn't complain, not really. Sally kept talking about Bobby, but she said he was somewhere else.

"Bobby gone away," she kept saying. "Gone far away."

I believed her. I thought it was all over, that we were safe.

What a fool. I should have known better. I

should have known they were waiting for a chance, a chance to make us part of the house.

A chance to make us dead, like them.

One night when I was least expecting it, I woke up abruptly out of a sound sleep.

Something had disturbed me. But what?

I sat up. A little moonlight filtered in through the window, turning everything silvery. It was late, very late.

"Jason."

It was Sally's voice calling. She was right outside my door and she sounded upset, frightened.

I jumped out of bed, grabbed the flashlight I always left on the night table, and flung open the door, ready to scoop my kid sister into my arms.

But it wasn't Sally.

A tall figure stood outside my door. It was shrouded from head to foot in shapeless black. A black hood covered where the face should be.

Slowly the hood moved. It was looking right at me. Out of the hood stared a white skull. A dead white skull with deep black holes for eyes!

The skeleton's skull jaws opened and an awful hiss emerged, pouring over me with the stench of the grave.

It tried to grab me. A sticklike arm came out of the sleeve and reached out. I ducked away but the thing knocked the flashlight out of my hand.

Stiffly the thing swung toward me again, staggering into my room.

I let out a yell, dove past it into the hallway and tried to run. But the thing enveloped me with folds of material. It had me. The black stuff draped around my head, blinding me.

I smelled sour earth and mold. The smell of a dead thing.

I flailed around but I couldn't get hold of anything solid. Then I tripped on the black shroud and rolled away, getting clear.

Suddenly fresh air streamed into my lungs. I was free! I crawled away, thinking only about escape. Behind me I heard the whisper of cloth, the sound of bones creaking as they rubbed together, coming after me.

I was in the hallway. I felt around and located the post at the top of the stairs. Escape! I could run down the stairs and out of the house and never stop running. Get away from this awful thing, this awful house, and never look back.

But I hesitated. I had to get Sally.

But how? I couldn't lead this thing to my little sister. She was safe in her room — for now at least.

Mom and Dad, then. I had to get to them, wake them up. But my heart sank. I knew they wouldn't be able to see the skeleton that had come to get me, or to scare me away so it could get Sally.

They didn't see any of the things that happened in this house. They would just send me back to bed and it would come for me again.

No, I had to fight it myself. Maybe there was something downstairs I could use as a weapon.

But I had hesitated too long.

I heard a low cackle, felt its rotten breath on the back of my neck. It was catching up. It reached for me.

I yelled and flung myself toward the stairs. I reached to catch hold of the banister but missed.

My hands grabbed nothing but air. Then my back hit the top of the stairs. I was rolling.

My head slammed the edge of a stair and everything went black.

25

The bang on the head stunned me for only a second — long enough for me to tumble halfway down the stairs. A jolt of pain woke me up as I bounced from one stair to the next and landed at the bottom.

I sat up and rubbed my head. Ouch! A nasty lump was forming.

All around me was darkness and quiet. The thing in the black shroud had not followed me down the stairs. No sound came from upstairs. Was the gruesome thing gone?

I tried squinting up the stairway, but I couldn't see a thing. It was so dark. Cautiously I looked around, peering into the shadowed dimness of the living room and the dining room. Nothing moved. Could the nightmare be over?

Gritting my teeth, I started back up the stairs. My plan was to check in on Sally, stay and guard her for the rest of the night.

I got up just one step.

Without warning something heavy flew over my head and crashed into the wall. As if that was a signal, the house erupted like a volcano, objects flying everywhere.

I covered my head with my arms and crouched low. I heard the lamp slide off the hall table and fly up. A second later the table followed, smashing the lamp in midair. A chair hurtled in from the dining table and crashed against the banister just above my head.

Vases and figurines flew off the shelf upstairs and collided with candlesticks and lamps from downstairs.

I peeked out from under my arms and saw a toy boat hurl itself at a silver serving tray from the dining room. *Wham-smash!* They were both destroyed.

I watched in horror as one of the heavy living room chairs rolled slowly toward me. It flipped end over end, smashed into the sofa, which shot up as if weightless, and then wedged itself in the doorway.

But how could I see what was going on? A moment ago it had been totally dark. Wait — there was a ghostly shimmering light over everything. I raised my head a fraction to try to find the source of the light. A heavy book zeroed in on my head. I ducked and the book slammed into the mirror behind me, exploding in a tinkly shower of glass.

I had to get out of here.

Cautiously I looked up again. The light seemed to be coming from upstairs. A soup ladle whizzed past my ear. I flinched away but not before I saw something move in the shadows at the top of the stairs.

My eyes searched the gloom beyond the light. There *was* something — someone — up there.

Two figures appeared in the ghostly light. One was tall, shrouded, and menacing — the thing that had come for me in my room. The other shape looked small and helpless, like a child. The weird, shimmery light swirled around their feet like glowing fog.

Suddenly the smaller shape broke away and tried to run toward me. But the tall thing grabbed it and held it back.

"Jason," cried the child. *"Jason, help me! Help me!"*

It was Sally, and the tall thing had her in its skeleton hands.

26

The sound of my sister's frightened cry made me leap up. I had to help her, no matter what.

The weird light flickered and beckoned me up the stairs. The two figures at the top struggled. I had to go to my sister. I had to save her!

But the thing had fooled me before with Sally's voice. Maybe it wasn't really her.

I hesitated and Sally cried out again, in pain this time. She twisted away but the skeleton thing had tight hold of her. "Jason!"

Sally's voice pierced my heart. I knew it was really Sally this time. I could feel it.

I gulped back my fear. The storm of flying objects was subsiding. A candlestick dropped abruptly to the floor and rolled lifelessly into a corner.

The evil that awaited me at the top of the stairs was far worse than a bunch of flying objects. I wanted to crawl into a corner and scream for my parents. Let them handle this, or make it go away. But would they ever hear me?

Now or never, Jason. Just do it.

I clenched my jaw and bolted up the stairs to Sally.

The ghostly light blazed brighter as I ran into it. But where was Sally? I whirled one way, then the other, reaching out. Both figures had disappeared.

And something was very wrong.

The hallway was different. The doors weren't where they should be. Sally's room was gone.

And the hall stretched without end into blackness.

I ran to the nearest door and turned the handle. Locked. I ran to the next and the next and the next. All locked. I ran back, banging on the doors and calling for Sally.

Chest heaving, I slumped against the wall, defeated. I didn't know what to do next. How would I ever find my little sister? How could I help if I couldn't get to her?

A sound jerked me to attention again. A pattering sound from the farthest, blackest part of the hall. It was coming closer. Footsteps, I realized.

A child's footsteps, running toward me, and coming faster.

"Sally?"

I stepped out into the center of the hall. I could hear a child's frightened breathing. The little footsteps pounded as hard as they could go.

Behind them came heavier steps. The child was being chased!

My breath quickened. Something terrible was about to happen! I started forward, seeking the sound of the frightened child, determined to help. I took a step and something slammed into me, knocking me over. But there was nothing there, nothing to see.

Now the invisible footsteps were flying past me, heading for the stairs.

The ghostly light blazed brighter again and a voice came out of it, screeching with evil. *"Give me that thing! It's mine, all mine! Give it to me now! Right now or else I'll — "*

A child screamed in terror. It hit me like a punch in the gut. The terrified scream increased, then trailed off. The scream of a child falling, falling a long way down.

Falling forever into the darkness.

The eerie light slowly faded. Silence fell over the house like a shroud. A terrible, terrible silence.

27

My whole body was trembling. I knew the falling child wasn't Sally but my dread was deeper than ever. Something terrible had happened here, and it made the whole house into a twisted, haunted place.

I rose on shaky legs. I was almost standing when the floor tilted sharply. My feet flew out from under me and my fingers scrabbled at the smooth floorboards, trying to get a grip.

But there was nothing to hold on to. Nothing to stop my downhill slide. I pressed my heels and hands into the floor but that only made me slide faster.

The whole house was tilting! It was aiming me at the dark end of the hallway. As I got closer, sliding faster and faster, I saw a door at the end of the hall.

It looked like an ordinary door but it was closed, and I was hurtling straight for it, going faster every second with no way to stop.

No way to stop.

I tensed my body and closed my eyes and a heartbeat later I crashed right through the door and came to a skidding stop in the middle of the room.

I got up slowly, aching all over, and looked around. I'd never seen this room before. It was small and bare with no windows.

Behind me the door slammed shut. I whirled around. The door had disappeared. Just four pale, seamless walls, barely visible in the dark.

I was trapped, with no way to escape.

But wait! As I stared in horror at the smooth walls, a sliver of light appeared through a crack in the corner. A way out!

I didn't care if it was a trap. I had to get out. I ran my fingers along the crack, feeling carefully for the outline of a door. It had to be there! Nothing. I felt along the floor but everything was smooth.

Was it my imagination or was the light along the crack starting to dim? "No," I cried out, and beat my fists against the wall.

I heard a click, felt something give way, and jumped back just as a section of the wall fell forward.

On the other side of the wall was a narrow winding stairway, glowing with faint, cold light. Stairs to nowhere.

As much as I wanted to escape this room, I was

never going to climb those stairs. No way. There was something terrible waiting for me up there, I just knew it.

A cold wind sprang up behind me, pushing me toward the stairs. I dug in my heels but the wind was strong and relentless. It pushed me inch by inch toward the opening.

I twisted to get away but the force of the wind turned me back. I was shivering with cold and terror. I braced my hands against the wall on either side of the opening and held on.

The wind was strong, but not strong enough to blow me up the stairs.

I'd beaten it.

Then I heard a faint cry, carried on the wind. "Jason!"

It was Sally. With a sinking sensation, I realized the cry was coming from the top of the stairway.

"Jason, help me, I'm scared," wailed Sally. "Jason, please."

I had to go. I was her only chance.

28

As I stepped over the threshold my feet felt like they weighed a thousand pounds. It was as if I was wading through an ocean of my own fear.

"Jason."

Sally's voice was very faint, getting smaller. I had to hurry. The stairs felt funny under my feet — sort of slippery and spongy. It was hard to get traction.

There was nothing to hold on to but the walls on either side. And the stairs were so steep and narrow.

My foot slipped. I started to go down and caught myself on the stairs with my hands.

I jerked back as if I'd been burned. The surface of the steps felt soft and cold and clammy — like dead human skin!

The stairway was alive.

I forced myself up the last few stairs, gasping for breath. The small door at the top was open.

The door was so low I had to stoop to get inside.

I was in the attic. But not a part I'd ever seen before.

Something told me this room didn't really exist. Not anymore. It was as the attic had been years before. It was as if I'd stepped back in time.

It was the room of a small child. There was a painted wooden rocking horse, a small iron bed, and a rocking chair. The room smelled stale, as if the air was a hundred years old. A cold creepiness tickled up my spine.

Then the rocking chair began to rock. It was facing the other way and I couldn't see who — or what — was in the chair.

It rocked to and fro, to and fro.

"Come to me," said a faint unrecognizable voice from the shadowy depths of the chair. *"Come to me, Jason. Come to me or die!"*

29

More than anything I wanted to run out of that strange little room and never look back. I didn't want to know what was in that rocking chair. I didn't care, all I wanted to do was get out of there.

But I couldn't leave Sally.

The house kept trying to trick me, trying to scare me. It didn't want me to find my little sister. It wanted her all to itself.

Something told me that if I ran down the stairs the house would let me back into my own room. I could sleep safe in my own bed. But I'd have to leave my sister behind.

I couldn't do that.

I opened my eyes. The little chair was still rocking there in the dark, in the shadows.

I had to know. Dread seeped into my veins as I crept toward the chair.

It kept rocking, *creeeek, creeeek, creeeeeek.*

I stretched out my hand, hestitated, then spun the chair around.

"Sally!"

It was my little sister. She was slumped in the chair, her blond curls covering her face.

I knelt on the floor and touched her shoulder. "Sally!"

She stirred, raised her head. I held my breath. Was she all right?

Sally opened her eyes, yawned, and smiled at me. I hugged her.

"Sally, how did you get here?"

She snuggled in my arms. "I don't know," she said, puzzlement in her voice. "I went to sleep and when I woked up I was in that little bed. It's Bobby's bed."

"You don't remember getting up here?"

Sally shook her head. "Bobby wants me to do something. But I didn't know what to do so I just got up and rocked in the chair. I knew you would come and save me."

I looked around and held Sally tighter. "What about Bobby? Is he here?"

Sally pushed away from me and looked around. "No. I don't think he is. He's in trouble."

"Trouble? What kind of trouble?" I asked.

"He wants us to save him," Sally said, looking at me with her big blue eyes.

"Save him from what?"

129

"I don't know." Sally clutched my arm with her little hand. "Something terrible."

Behind me the floorboards creaked heavily. Something had come into the room. I thrust Sally behind me and turned around to face it.

The grandfather clock was standing in the doorway.

How did it get all the way up here?

The clock struck the hour. The sound echoed in the small, low-ceilinged room. Three times it struck.

When the echo died out, a metallic, mechanical voice began to speak from inside the clock.

"TICK TICK TICK," it said. "YOUR TIME IS UP!"

Sally clung to me, hiding her face in my pajama top.

The clock began to creep toward us across the floor, shuffling and rocking.

Coming to get us.

I backed up until I was against the wall with no place to go.

The big clock loomed over us, then tipped forward. It started to topple.

Its weight would crush us like bugs!

30

I crouched over Sally, waiting for the clock to smash us to pieces. Suddenly I felt a cold breeze — there was a crack in the floor, right under us!

I felt around and found a metal ring set into the floor — the handle of a trapdoor! I had no idea where it went, but it didn't matter. If we stayed here we'd be roadkill.

So I twisted the handle on the trapdoor and it opened. Sally and I fell through the hole and the clock landed with a crash across the opening, just missing us.

As we fell I hugged Sally tight, bracing for impact. To my surprise we landed on something soft and bounced.

I opened my eyes and looked around. We were on Sally's own bed, in Sally's own room.

Above us the trapdoor slammed closed. Then it vanished and the ceiling was smooth again.

A howl of rage came from the attic above. There

was a furious pounding on the ceiling and we were showered with plaster and dust.

Sally whimpered in fear and I held her until the noise stopped.

Around us the house quieted.

I stayed huddled on the bed, thinking. Trying to concentrate. Something had saved us from the evil clock. Was it Bobby? But Sally said it was Bobby who took her to the attic in the first place. Just as it was Bobby who put her in the tree — and then saved her from falling. So maybe Bobby had somehow saved us from the evil clock. Maybe he was trying to help, somehow, and wanted us to help him in return.

But what about the skeleton in black that stalked me and wandered the house searching for something? Who was that? What did it want? Why was it threatening us?

Whatever it was, its presence seemed to bring out the demon in Bobby.

I sighed and peeled Sally off me. She was still pretty scared. "I think we're safe now, Sally," I said. "But we have to get out of this house. At least until morning."

"I want Mommy," said Sally. "I want my mommy."

OK," I said. "We'll wake up Mommy. But first let's get a sweater on you in case we have to go outside."

My heart finally began to slow to normal as the house stayed quiet. Maybe Sally and I had just gotten caught in the middle of a struggle between Bobby and the skeleton thing. Maybe they had finished their battle in the attic and it was over, for tonight, at least.

I wanted desperately to believe it was over but I was still as jumpy as a cat. I got up from the bed and moved very quietly to Sally's dresser to get her a sweater. When the shadow of a branch crossed the window I almost leaped out of my skin.

I took the sweater back to Sally and helped her put it on. "All right. Let's go wake up Mom and Dad," I said, gathering up Sally and reaching behind me for the door handle while keeping an eye on the window.

My searching hand met nothing but smooth wall. I spun around. The door was gone. I stared in sinking disbelief.

Behind me came strange, gleeful laughter. I stiffened, afraid to turn.

There was something in the room with us! The laughter came from everywhere. It had a speeded-up, unreal sound, like cartoon laughter from the television. Sally began to wail and I turned slowly around. My jaw dropped when I saw what it was.

All of Sally's toys had come to life. They were

looking at us and laughing. Laughing like evil, evil creatures.

The wooden pull-toy duck in the corner was flapping its bill. The clown puppet's mouth was a round red "O" as it screamed an insane laugh. The jack-in-the-box sprang up and bounced with a tinny *tee-hee-hee*. Three dolls put their heads together and giggled like mad demons. Even Sally's crayons danced with mean-spirited glee.

Only Winky the rabbit lay quietly on her pillow, looking sad.

Sally hid her face in my shoulder. "Make them stop," she whimpered. "Jason, please make them stop."

I put her down gently on her bed, then began grabbing the toys and throwing them into her closet. Each toy hiccupped when it hit the wall and fell to the floor laughing crazily. I wanted to get them all, make them all shut up. I scrambled on hands and knees, grabbing every last one of the nasty things and tossing them all into the closet.

I was surprised how good it made me feel to be throwing things rather than having them thrown at me. Take that, you stupid toys! I shut the closet door with a sigh, then whirled at a choking sound behind me.

I'd missed one of the toys.

The clown puppet had come to life. It had grown

long, rubber fingers and wrapped them tight around her neck. It was strangling Sally.

My sister's eyes rolled as she struggled. Her small arms pushed at the clown but it held on, grinning with evil.

She tried to scream but the clown had squeezed off her air.

31

I dove for Sally. I yanked at the clown but the toy dragged Sally after it.

I wedged my fingers under the rubber clown fingers and pried at them. Sally's neck felt so small and fragile, I was afraid of hurting her myself.

I had to get her free or she'd die.

The clown squeezed harder. It grinned an evil smile at me. I was frantic. I forced myself to calm down and concentrate all my strength on my fingers.

Finally I broke the puppet's grip and smashed it against the wall. As it hit the wall all the laughter abruptly stopped.

It wasn't over.

The room suddenly got cold. The temperature dropped swiftly and Sally's teeth were soon chattering. It was like the North Pole in there! I grabbed the blanket off her bed and wrapped us both in it. I was shivering, too, fighting off the incredible cold.

Ice formed on the window and our breath filled the room with fog. I felt around under the bed for Sally's sweater and brought it under the blanket.

"Here, Sally, let's get this on you." She was already stiff with cold and I had to lift each of her arms to get the sweater on.

The instant I let go of the blanket it flew off. The blanket fluttered about the room. As it settled, a small form took shape under it.

I could make out a head, shoulders — it was a child!

Noises started to come from under the blanket as if whoever was huddled under it was trying to speak.

"Can you hear what he's saying, Sally?" I asked. "Is that Bobby?"

But Sally was shivering too much to pay attention to anything.

The little figure continued to move around under the blanket, struggling to make itself heard. But I couldn't make out a word.

It was Bobby — who else could it be? And this was my chance to catch him and find out what he wanted. Find out why he was haunting the house.

I waited until the shape came close to Sally's bed, then pounced, arms outstretched.

I landed on the floor on an empty blanket. The apparition had vanished.

I lay there for a second, feeling totally defeated.

Until Sally shouted excitedly. "Look! The doors!"

32

I sat up. A second ago we'd been trapped in a room that had no doors. Now it had too many. There was a row of doors running the length of the wall.

The house was trying to trick us again, but I was pretty sure I knew which one was the real door, Sally's old door.

"Stay there, Sally," I said. "While I check."

I went to the familiar-looking door and reached for the knob.

It sprouted teeth and snapped at my fingers.

I whipped my hand back and jumped away.

I realized this was a sort of test. We *might* find the way out — if I chose the right door.

But how would I know?

I could start by touching the doorknobs and seeing what happened. Not with my hand, of course — I didn't want to get my fingers chomped off. I looked around for something to use.

Sally's baton. She was too little to learn how to twirl it, anyway. I grabbed the baton and went to the first door. No, the right door would never be the first door. Too obvious.

I took a deep breath and, before I could lose my nerve, reached out with the baton and touched the knob of the second door.

Nothing happened.

I pushed at the knob until it clicked. The door opened and sunlight filled the room. Green grass sloped down to the pine trees. My heart leaped for joy — we could escape to the backyard.

"Come on, Sally," I cried. "We're out of here!"

I picked her up from the bed and started through the door.

With one foot over the threshold, I hesitated.

Wait a minute. It was sunny out there. But it should be dark. It was night, it was supposed to be dark.

My foot sank down into empty space. I jumped back and the vision of the sunny backyard winked out in an instant. On the other side of the door loomed a dark, vast, bottomless pit.

And we'd almost fallen for it — fallen right into it!

I slammed the door and stood there shaking, clutching hold of Sally.

"That was a close one," I muttered. "How do I decide which one to try next?"

I sat down on the bed with Sally, and tried to think it through. Which door? One of them led to safety, I would stake my life on it.

The house wasn't going to wait for me to make up my mind. The room started to shake. Then the bed tipped and threw us to the floor.

Sally started to cry. The air grew thick with menace. Something was coming to get us. Something worse than anything we'd seen so far.

We had to get out. But which door?

33

Sally yanked at my arm. "Come on, Jason, I want to go," she cried. "Look!"

One of the doors opened slowly, as if pushed by an invisible hand.

"Get me out of here, Jason, please!" cried Sally, tugging me along.

The floor bucked harder, as if trying to prevent us from reaching the open door.

All that showed on the other side of the door was blackness. I couldn't see a thing. We might be leaving this terrible place for something worse. I pulled Sally back.

"It's Bobby," cried Sally, trying to wriggle out of my arms. I clutched her tighter. "He says we should hurry."

The room shook us like dice in a cup. I couldn't hold on to Sally. She got away from me and ran to the door.

"Sally, no!" I cried.

How could we trust Bobby? It was Bobby who'd

taken Sally to the attic. Sure, he'd also provided the trapdoor in the nick of time but then he had imprisoned us in this room. He wanted to keep Sally with him forever, I was sure of it.

Sally hesitated at the door, looking back at me. "Come on, Jason, it's all right," she pleaded. She stumbled back to me over the heaving floor and grabbed my hand. "Come on."

Her eyes were shining. Sally truly believed that Bobby would rescue us. Maybe she was right. And what other chance did we have, anyway?

As I started to rise, the floor bucked and I went down on one knee, hard. Sally helped me up and I followed her to the open door.

Now or never. This might be the end for both of us. We'd be trapped for eternity.

I held Sally's hand tight as we stepped through the door into the darkness.

Suddenly we were on a winding stairway, going down. There was just enough light to see the next step. I couldn't tell where we were going but Sally kept trying to skip ahead of me, giddy with relief to be out of her haunted room.

My throat was tight with fear. The stairs seemed to go on forever. Where was Bobby taking us?

A child's laughter floated up from somewhere below. My stomach clenched at the sound, but Sally joined in, laughing as if all this was a delightful game.

The smell of green grass and pine came drifting up the stairs. It smelled clean and safe and real. A part of me started to hope our night of terror was over. Sally pulled at me to go faster.

We reached the bottom. Another door stood open and a fresh breeze beckoned.

Still hesitant, I moved cautiously forward. I poked my head out the doorway.

We were in the backyard! For real, this time.

"Go to the tree," whispered a child's voice beside my ear. *"You'll be safe by the tree."*

I jumped and looked all around but I couldn't see anybody there.

"Come on, Jason," Sally demanded, hopping up and down.

I let Sally lead the way to the cherry tree. I looked back at the house and was startled to see a little boy standing in the doorway we'd just come through.

A little boy. And I could see right through him.

The child waved and smiled and then the boy and the doorway both vanished.

Sally lay down on the grass under the cherry tree and was asleep in an instant. I was still awake and guarding her when the sun broke over the horizon.

We had survived.

34

A cold hand gripped my shoulder. I bolted upright, instantly alert. "Mom!"

Sally rubbed her eyes and blinked in the sunshine.

"You two gave me a fright," said Mom, sounding really worried. "I checked your rooms this morning and you weren't there. What are you *doing* out here?"

Dad appeared over her shoulder. "Well?" he said. "Is this some kind of game, Jason?"

Why were they acting like everything was normal?

"Is everything all right inside?" I asked. "Anything broken?"

"What?" said Dad, looking puzzled. "Of course everything's all right. What shouldn't be all right?"

"I don't know," I mumbled, thinking of the overturned furniture, smashed mirrors and vases and lamps, broken crockery. I should have known it would all be back in place now, because the house didn't want my parents to know what was going on.

Dad took me aside. He looked stern. "If you're frightening your sister with this ghost nonsense, I'll be very disappointed in you, young man," he said.

I knew it was no use trying to tell them what had happened. They'd think I was making it up.

Mom bent down to Sally's level. "What were you scared of, honey? Was it Bobby?"

Sally looked at me and pushed out her lower lip. "I'm not scared of Bobby," she said stoutly. "Bobby is my friend."

"She, ah, she had a nightmare," I said. "I woke up and it was hot, so we decided to come out for a minute. I guess we fell asleep."

Mom sighed and stood up. "Let's go in and have breakfast."

"Nightmares are hungry business," said Dad, scooping up Sally and putting her on his shoulders. She squealed with glee as he trotted toward the house, playing horse.

Now it was Mom's turn to look stern and serious. "It isn't more of this ghost business, is it, Jason? I don't want to be worrying about you while we're gone."

I stopped in my tracks and stared at her. "Gone? Where are you going?"

"We got a call late last night," said Mom. "Remember that firehouse we designed for Mayfield last spring? Apparently they're having some problems with construction and they need us to go take a look at the site and make some changes."

"You have to leave?"

Mom nodded. "We'll be gone a week or so and we have to leave today — as soon as possible. But I don't want to leave you here if you're scared."

"Scared? Of course I'm not scared." That was partly true. I wasn't scared when I was outside the house, in broad daylight. "I'm just, ah, I'm worried about Sally and her invisible playmate."

Mom smiled. "Then I can trust you to keep a close eye on her while we're gone?"

"Sure, Mom. Of course you can."

"Good. Then let's eat before the baby-sitter gets here."

"Baby-sitter?"

Mom gave me a look. "I know you're getting pretty big, Jason, but I still can't leave you to handle a five-year-old all by yourself. The baby-sitter's name is Katie. She's seventeen and she comes highly recommended."

The last thing I wanted was a bossy baby-sitter, but as I followed Mom into the house I tried to convince myself that maybe it wasn't such a bad thing after all.

Mom and Dad would never let me and Sally camp out under the cherry tree every night. But maybe I could talk the baby-sitter into it.

Maybe *she'd* believe me.

35

The baby-sitter, Katie Lawrence, had kind of skinny legs but other than that she was pretty. Her hair was red and thick and came down to her shoulders. She had this little sprinkling of freckles on her nose and she smiled a lot.

She grinned at me when we were introduced and she didn't seem bothered by the fact that Sally was scowling at her.

I showed her around the house while my parents finished packing. Wouldn't you know, all the rooms looked sunny and pleasant in the late morning light. You'd never know what had happened the night before, or what was likely to happen again, as soon as the sun went down.

"What a neat old place," said Katie as we came back downstairs. "I always wanted to see what this house looked like on the inside. It was shut up for so many years we used to dare each other to come here on Halloween."

"Did anything ever happen?" I asked carefully. "On Halloween, I mean."

Katie's laughter rang out. "Of course not, silly. Although we never did anything more than run up and peek in the windows. I thought I saw a light one time," she added, winking at me. "Like a candle, flickering in the attic."

Just then my dad called me upstairs to help with the suitcases.

We loaded the suitcases into the station wagon and when we got back to the house Mom was giving Sally a hug and going over instructions with Katie one last time.

"Don't hesitate to call us if there's any problem," she said again.

Dad cocked an eyebrow at Katie. "You don't believe in ghosts, do you?" he asked with a smile.

Katie giggled. "No, of course not. There's no such thing as ghosts. Why? Is this house haunted?"

She laughed like it was a pretty good joke.

"Jason thinks so," said Dad, giving me a look. "But maybe you can convince him."

I felt my face going red.

I said good-bye to Mom and Dad and they climbed into the car. I held Sally's hand as they drove away.

A moment later the car turned the corner and they were gone.

Katie went back into the house, saying she wanted to unpack her things. "You know, there *is* something spooky about this house," she called back. "I think I'm going to really like it here!"

I shivered at her carefree tone. We were on our own. Just me and Sally and a new baby-sitter who thought ghosts were cool.

And I was the only one who knew what was going on. Or did I, really?

I turned to Sally and smiled comfortingly. "You and me better keep an eye on that baby-sitter, make sure she doesn't get in any trouble she can't handle, right?"

That's when I noticed that something was wrong with Sally's face. Her expression was stiff and her eyes were blank. As if she was in a trance or something.

A chill ran through me.

"Sally?" My voice was shaky.

Sally's head jerked to one side and then the other, like a puppet. Her eyes smoldered and glowed.

I fought the urge to leap away from her.

Then she opened her mouth and spoke. *"I'm not Sally."*

The voice that came out of her mouth was rough, as if it hadn't been used in a long time.

And it had a hollow ring. As if it was coming from the inside of an empty tomb.

Sally's face scowled at me and the strange voice growled again. "My name is Bobby," she said. "And I've been dead for a long time."

I was paralyzed. I wanted to run. I wanted to scream.

My little sister was possessed.

Don't Miss
THE HOUSE ON CHERRY STREET
Book II: *The Horror*

The next thing I knew there was a blue light shining in my eyes.

I was too late. It had started.

My room was filled with silvery light. A cold, cold light that made my skin look pale blue, like a corpse's.

The light was coming out of my closet! No, not the closet. The mirror on the closet door. The mirror was glowing.

A strange, glowing cloud swirled in the center of the mirror.

It was getting thicker, spinning faster and faster. I couldn't stop staring. I tried closing my eyes but I couldn't. It was like the mirror was hypnotizing me, sucking me in.

The cloud darkened. It was taking shape.

A picture was forming in the mirror!

It was a room. I almost recognized it. Almost — then the cloud dissolved into mist again, swirling and plucking at me.

I sat up, moving like a zombie.

The mist in the mirror came together. It formed

the image of a bedroom. A room right here in the house.

My sister must be in danger!

I tried getting up — I wanted to run in and check on her — But suddenly I couldn't move a muscle. I could only stare into the mirror as the picture became clearer and more detailed.

Slowly a bed swam into view, then a long, black shape. The shape grew darker and sharper.

It was the old lady, the skeleton thing shrouded in black.

And it wasn't Sally's bedroom, it was my baby-sitter Katie's room! I recognized her four-poster bed and the flowered wallpaper and could even see a dark blob that must be her head on the pillow.

In the mirror the old witch-thing was bending over Katie.

I watched helplessly as a long, bony claw reached out — sharp, bony fingers stretching toward Katie's sleeping head.

Then suddenly there was a popping sound and the mirror flashed and went blank.

My room was plunged into total darkness.

From somewhere in the house came a long, piercing shriek of terror.

"Aaahhhheeeee!"

The scream was cut off.

But the house was not quiet. No, the house wasn't quiet at all.

About the Authors

RODMAN PHILBRICK is the author of numerous mysteries and suspense stories for adults, and the much-acclaimed Young Adult novel *Freak the Mighty*. LYNN HARNETT is an award-winning journalist and a founding editor of *Kidwriters Monthly*. The husband-and-wife writing team divide their time between Kittery, Maine, and the Florida Keys.

High on a hill,
trapped in the shadows,
something inside a dark house
is waiting...and watching.

THE HOUSE ON CHERRY STREET

**A three-book series
by Rodman Philbrick and Lynn Harnett**

Terror has a new home—and the children are
the only ones who sense it—from the blasts of
icy air in the driveway, to the windows that shut
like guillotines. Can Jason and Sally stop the evil
that lives in the dark?

**Book #1: THE HAUNTING
Book #2: THE HORROR
Book #3: THE FINAL NIGHTMARE**

HCS1194